Corgi Capers:

The Sorceress of Stoney Brook

Val Muller

ALL RIGHTS RESERVED

Publishers Note:

This is a work of fiction. All names, characters, places, and events are the work of the author's imagination. Any resemblance to real persons, places, or events is coincidental.

Cover Art: Justin James

ISBN 13: 978-0615707792
ISBN 10: 0615707793

D W B   P U B L I S H I N G
CHILDReNS LINe
www.dwbchildrensline.com

Dedication

To Lisa—for turning on the lights when I was afraid.

Acknowledgements

Sincere thanks to my parents for their constant support during my childhood; to my husband for his editorial eye and business acumen; to my publisher Marie McGaha for her faith in my stories; to my good friend Voula Trip, of Voula Trip Photography, for the photos; to my test readers for their feedback: Madison McKay, Erin Plowman, Joanna Plowman, and Ryan D'Onofrio; and to my muses, Leia the growly-monster, and Yoda the fraidy-dog.

~ ONE ~
The Stranger

A corgi barked from the kitchen window as Coach Harris's pick-up truck pulled into the driveway. Adam Hollinger stepped out of the truck and waved up at the kitchen window.

"Hi Zeph," he shouted. Adam slung a school bag over one shoulder and a baseball bag over the other. "Bye, Patrick," Adam yelled as the truck pulled away.

Patrick Harris was the coach's son and Adam's best friend. Their All-Star baseball team, the Lancaster Reds, practiced hard every day after school. They were determined to win the Autumn League State Championship.

Adam turned to see the cool October sun disappearing behind the hill of Mr. Frostburg's house. Or rather, the house in which Mr. Frostburg *used* to live. Ever since Adam and his corgi, Zeph, caught Mr. Frostburg burglarizing neighborhood homes, no one had seen Mr. Frostburg. He'd been arrested, and Mr. Hollinger said it might be a long time before anyone saw the likes of him.

For the past month, a large 'For Rent' sign stood near the end of the driveway, and the house remained vacant. Adam always got the creeps when he looked at that empty house, but this time was even scarier than usual. On the front porch that used to belong to Mr. Frostburg, stood a robed and hooded figure. When the wind blew, the robe lifted and swirled so that the figure seemed to hover like a ghost. The wind flicked the robe, and a strand of long, blonde hair came loose from the hood, blowing like a kite tail in the wind. Then the hood blew back over the figure, shrouding it in shadow. Adam closed his eyes and counted to three. When he opened them again, the figure was gone.

Adam raced the setting rays of the sun into his house, where Zeph barreled down the stairs to greet him. Zeph's happy howl made Adam forget—at least for now—the strange figure on the hill.

"Where's Sapphie?" Adam asked Zeph. "Not in trouble again, I hope."

Zeph wagged his stubby tail and ran up the stairs, beckoning Adam to follow.

Upstairs, Adam and Zeph stopped in front of Courtney's bedroom door. Courtney, Adam's older sister, was a seventh-grader now. Ever since school started, she spent most of her time in her room with the door closed.

Zeph barked and scratched on Courtney's door.

"What do you want, stupid?" Courtney asked, opening her door only a crack.

At the bottom of the door, a tiny nose poked out. It was Sapphie's. She sniffed and cried and clawed at the door until Courtney let her out. Sapphie jumped high in the air, springing into Adam's arms. Zeph barked jealously as Sapphie licked Adam's ear.

"Mom's gonna be so mad," Courtney said.

"Why?" asked Adam.

"When she sees what you look like, she'll be mad—with the new neighbor coming over."

"What new neighbor? And what do you mean, *what I look like*?"

"Ever heard of a mirror?"

Courtney flung her door wide open and pointed to a full-length mirror on the wall. Adam looked beyond the magazine clippings of celebrities that decorated the mirror and examined his reflection.

His sweatpants were dusty from running drills. Coach spent most of practice making the team work on base running and sliding. Adam's face was scuffed with white chalk from the pitcher's mound and his red hair—now covered in dust—stuck straight up, as if he'd rubbed it with a balloon.

"Don't you know anything? There's a new neighbor moving into Mister Frostburg's old house." Courtney said. "Mom invited her over for dinner, and we're supposed to look nice and be polite."

Adam glanced at his sister. Courtney's face looked like she had covered it in makeup and tried to rub it off when she heard Adam coming. Adam started to question her about it but then changed his mind.

"Have you seen the new neighbor yet?" Adam asked. "I was coming home from practice, I looked over, and I saw a really weird…"

But before Adam could finish, Mrs. Hollinger came up the stairs carrying Adam's school bag. Her eyes widened when she saw Adam.

"You've got to get cleaned up," she scolded. "Miss Arabella will be here soon, and I want you looking your best."

"Who's Miss Arabella?" Adam asked.

But Mrs. Hollinger didn't answer. She was too busy pushing him into the bathroom, shoving a stack of towels and washcloths into his hands. Mrs. Hollinger closed the bathroom door on him before he had a chance to protest.

~ TWO ~
The Only Thing Worse than Asparagus

When Adam came downstairs after his shower, everyone was already seated at the table. Zeph and Sapphie sat curiously in the kitchen right next to the child-safety gate, noses in the air, sniffing and hoping for a bite. Sapphie looked ready to burst.

As Adam descended the stairs, he smelled something strange. It reminded him of the meadows of wildflowers he hiked through with his scout group. When he entered the dining room, he saw the source seated at the head of the table. The guest's long, dark hair was tied back in a purple scarf. Silver earrings in the shape of oak leaves dangled from her ears. She reminded Adam of a gypsy from the black-and-white werewolf movies his dad liked to watch on rainy Saturdays.

"You must be Adam," she said, smiling. "Mrs. Hollinger told me all about you."

Adam's mother smiled. "You can call me Susan, dear."

The guest smiled and nodded. Then she stood and offered her hand. "I'm Arabella. Arabella Spinelli. But you can call me Belle."

"Nice to meet you, Miss Belle," Adam said, trying to be polite.

He shook her hand hesitantly. Every finger—even her thumb—was covered in elaborate rings. One of them had a big, red jewel in it. Another was shaped like oak leaves climbing up her finger. One even looked like a lizard wrapped around her thumb.

Adam tried not to stare, but he couldn't help it. Belle's outfit wasn't exactly what he considered normal. She wore a long, blue skirt decorated with dozens of beads reflecting the light as the skirt swayed in the draft. Her pale yellow shirt was elaborate and ruffled, and she wore three or four colorful necklaces. As she shook Adam's hand, dozens of bangle bracelets clattered in a cacophony of sound.

"We've been waiting for you, Adam," Courtney said, and folded her arms. "Mom said we couldn't eat till you got here. Nice of you to finally show up."

Adam felt his ears burn. "Sorry," he mumbled, looking at the dishes wrapped in foil. "Practice ran late."

"Who cares?" Courtney whined. "I'm hungry."

As soon as Mr. Hollinger removed the foil from the dishes, Adam could tell it was going to be a bad dinner. Mom made salmon and asparagus—Adam didn't like either one.

"Help yourself," Mrs. Hollinger said, passing a steaming plate of asparagus to the new guest.

Arabella Spinelli took a heaping helping of the disgusting vegetables and passed them to Adam.

"Asparagus?" She stared right into his eyes, the way a teacher does when you're not paying attention. Her eyes were bright green and reminded Adam of cat's eyes.

"Yuk," Adam grunted, taking the plate and passing it quickly to his sister.

"Adam," Mrs. Hollinger warned, arching one brow.

Adam took back the dish and glanced at Belle, who watched him place a few stalks on his plate. Her mouth curled into a smile.

"When I was a kid, I hated cauliflower," she said.

Courtney laughed. "Adam hates that, too. Adam, you'd better take more asparagus. If you don't eat your vegetables, how are you ever gonna win your game on Saturday? You know you'll never forgive yourself if York beats Lancaster," Courtney smirked, mocking her little brother.

Adam scowled and passed her the plate.

"I didn't know baseball ran this late in the year," said Belle.

"It's Autumn League," Adam said proudly, forgetting—for the time being—the creepy way Belle stared into his eyes. "It's a regional All-Star league, and it's the end of our season. Saturday's the next game in the play-offs. We're playing York. York and Lancaster are the two teams going for Southeast Regional champions. Then the four regions play for the title! We've just got to beat York."

"They're Lancaster's biggest rival," Mr. Hollinger added. "Around these parts, anyway."

Adam smiled. "And the final games in the playoffs is just twenty-four days away."

"*Are*," Mrs. Hollinger corrected quietly. "The final games *are* just twenty-four days away."

"If you make it that far," Courtney smirked. She passed the asparagus to her father without taking any herself.

"Well," Adam admitted, "we *do* have to make it through Saturday's game, and then play whoever gets to the next level..." Adam speared an asparagus stalk with his fork but thought better of it.

"I'm the pitcher," he said, trying to avoid eating the disgusting vegetable.

"The *relief* pitcher," Courtney corrected. "He's not good enough to be the *starting* pitcher."

"Now Courtney, that isn't nice," Mr. Hollinger said. "Adam gets to pitch at every game."

"Good for you, Adam," Belle said. She ate a piece of asparagus. "Delicious!"

Mrs. Hollinger smiled. "The kids don't really like asparagus, so I only make it when we have guests."

"Adam doesn't like it 'cause it makes your pee smell funny." Courtney giggled.

Adam's felt his ears heating again, and Belle looked down at her plate.

Courtney stopped laughing. "Why would you want to live in that creepy old house, anyway?" she asked.

"The rent is *very* reasonable. The landlord had to rent it rather quickly after the last tenant moved out, so he gave us a good deal. But more than that, I like the location," Belle said. "I love the old oak trees out back, and there's this great garden the former tenant completely ignored. I can't wait until spring."

"I'm sure Mister Frostburg was too busy scheming. He didn't have time for gardening," Mr. Hollinger said.

Courtney scowled. "I hate him," she mumbled.

"There's also a great living room where I like to do my schoolwork. The afternoon sunlight is so soothing. I can just read there for hours."

"Schoolwork at your age?" Courtney muttered, but only Adam heard.

"You must like reading," Adam said.

"Don't you?"

"I like comic books." Adam grabbed three dinner rolls, hoping to fill up on them rather than fish or asparagus.

"Maybe when you're older, you'll like other books as well."

"Not me," Courtney said. "I don't even like comic books. What in the world would a grown-up want with books or school?"

"I like reading books," Mrs. Hollinger reminded her daughter.

Courtney rolled her eyes. "That's because you're an editor, Mom. Why in the world would anyone else want to read books?"

"I love to read," Arabella said. "Besides that, I'm working on my Master's degree."

"What's that?" Adam asked.

"Once you finish elementary school, middle school, and high school," Arabella explained, "you can go on to college, and eventually, you can earn your Master's degree."

"That sounds like way too much homework," Courtney said. "As soon as I finish high school, I'm never gonna open another book again."

Mrs. Hollinger gave Courtney a look of disapproval. "*Going to,*" she corrected. "And you *are* going to if I have anything to say about it."

Courtney's cell phone beeped and she checked the screen.

"Courtney," Mr. Hollinger scolded. "No texting at the table, especially when we have a guest."

"Sorry," Courtney muttered, even though she didn't look sorry from what Adam could see.

While Mrs. Hollinger turned back to her plate, Courtney snuck her cell phone on her lap and sent a text reply. A strange smile lingered on her face for a few minutes, but only Adam seemed to notice.

"So Adam, I was wondering if you ever do yard work for your neighbors?" Arabella asked.

Adam stopped looking at his sister and nodded. "I made three hundred dollars this summer by watering plants and weeding while neighbors were on vacation. Next summer, Dad says I can start mowing lawns."

"Great," Arabella said. "I was hoping I could find someone to rake all the leaves in my yard. It seems like they never stop falling. With all my homework, and my new part-time job, I could use some help. Are you interested?"

Adam looked at his parents. Arabella sure was creepy, not to mention that she lived in Mr. Frostburg's old house. And who—or what—was that mysterious figure he'd seen earlier on her front porch?

"I think that's a wonderful idea," Mrs. Hollinger said.

"And I'd pay you, of course," Arabella said.

Adam frowned. "I'd like to but..." he stuttered, searching for an excuse. "I'm so busy with baseball practice and homework. I don't know if I'll have time."

"Nonsense, Adam," Mr. Hollinger said. "You can spare a few minutes to help a neighbor—"

"Besides, you'll make some extra spending cash," Mrs. Hollinger added.

"I think he's just scared of that yard," Courtney taunted. "It's getting to be Halloween and he's afraid Mister Frostburg's old place is haunted."

"No," Adam whispered, trying to forget the strange robed figure on the porch.

"You're afraid the ghooooost of Mister Froooostburg will get yoooou," Courtney moaned like a ghost, her fingers extended like claws, as she leaned toward him, and then cackled like a witch.

"Am not," Adam yelled, just a little too loudly for the dinner table.

Mrs. Hollinger scowled. "Courtney, there *is* no ghost, and Adam knows that. Let's all just settle down and have a nice dinner."

Adam looked down at his food and scowled at the pink piece of fish and wondered what was so "nice" about it.

Mr. Hollinger put down his fork. "Maybe Courtney has a point," he said. "Adam, if you feel uncomfortable at Mister Frostburg's old place, maybe Courtney can rake instead."

"No," Courtney squealed, and her face paled. "Adam isn't afraid. He can do the raking."

All eyes turned to Adam.

"I..." Adam wasn't sure what to say.

"You see," Mr. Hollinger explained to Arabella, "there's a history behind that house you just rented. I'm not sure how much you've heard about it, but this summer, the man who lived there broke into our house—along with the Pinkneys' house, the Stoys' house, and half a dozen others. He'd been living here for years, and no one suspected him. No one that is, except for Adam and the corgis."

From the kitchen, Zeph howled.

"A newspaper reporter even interviewed Adam about the incident. Though they never did print the story, did they?" Adam's mother looked at her husband.

"No," Mr. Hollinger replied. "They never did. And Poor Zeph got injured. Didn't you, Zeph?" Mr.

Hollinger asked the corgi, who still sat at the child safety gate, hoping for a tidbit.

Zeph barked once in reply. Sapphie didn't know why he was barking but she was happy to join in. She bounced up and down on her hind legs like a baby kangaroo and pounced on Zeph, biting his ear. Before long, the puppies were barking and scampering in circles in the kitchen. Adam wished he could play with them instead of finishing dinner. He'd rather eat *dog food* than fish and asparagus!

"I did hear something about all that," Arabella said, once the dogs quieted down. "It must have been scary when Mister Frostburg locked your puppies in his shed."

Adam raised one brow. He remembered Riley Couth, his favorite comic book detective, and how he always caught criminals when they revealed information they weren't supposed to know.

"How did you know they were locked in the shed?" Adam asked.

"Hmm," Arabella pondered. "I must have read it somewhere." She shrugged. "Anyway, if you're uncomfortable spending time in the backyard, I can always find someone else to rake."

"You'd better find someone else," Courtney said, looking at Adam. "My brother's the biggest chicken you'll ever meet."

"Am not," Adam said. "I'd be glad to rake leaves for you." He smiled defiantly. He had to prove Courtney wrong.

"Great," Arabella said. "And I'd love for you to bring Zeph along."

Adam looked away from Arabella's green eyes and tried to swallow the asparagus without tasting it. Almost immediately, he regretted agreeing to rake her leaves. A chill crawled up his spine as he remembered the strange, robed figure standing on Arabella's porch. He couldn't wait until dinner was over so he could play outside with Zeph—and get away from the strange new neighbor.

~ THREE ~
A Corgi Conversation

Meanwhile, in the kitchen, the puppies had settled down. Zeph sat on the floor panting, and Sapphie plopped down next to him.

"Adam sure looks uncomfortable," Zeph said.

"What do you mean? How can you be uncomfortable when you're eating? Eating is the best thing in the world," Sapphie cheered. "Except for sleeping, of course, and playing!"

"Not the way Adam's eating." Both dogs leaned forward to watch Adam eat. He seemed to chew only with his front teeth, like he didn't want the food to touch his tongue, and he scowled the whole time. "It doesn't look like he's enjoying his food."

"Whatever it is, I'd sure like some," Sapphie said. "You know what would be great? If you could sleep and eat at the *same time*. It would be the best of both worlds! Maybe I should try it..."

But Zeph wasn't listening. "Adam keeps looking suspiciously at that new person."

"What does *suspiciously* mean?" Sapphie asked.

"It means he isn't sure he can trust her. And if Adam isn't sure about her, then neither am I."

"I think she looks really nice," Sapphie said. "And those things on her arm make a delicious noise when she moves. And look at that purple thing on her head. It looks like it would be fun to chew, chew, *chew*!"

Zeph growled softly. "You can't chew on everything you see, Sapphie."

"I *don't*," Sapphie complained.

"Yes, you do."

"Name *one* thing I chewed on that I wasn't supposed to. I can do whatever I want because I'm cute, cute, *cute!*"

"Then what about when you chewed on Dad's slippers?" Zeph asked.

Sapphie rolled onto her back. "Those were his *old* slippers. I was doing him a favor. He got nice fluffy new ones after that."

"You chewed those, too. And how about that tube of Courtney's lip gloss? And Mom's favorite pens? Dozens of newspapers? And five or six socks? Do you even remember how much trouble you got into? Not to mention the time we ripped up Adam's comic book—"

Sapphie sprung from the floor and peered out the gate.

"I really want to chew on that purple thing. I'll steal it right off her head," Sapphie insisted. "Do you think she's going to come over here?"

"I doubt it," Zeph said.

"Let's jump over this gate, then." Sapphie barked and jumped all over her brother.

"No, Sapphie. We can't jump over the gate."

"Sure we can. Don't you remember the time we had to catch Mister Frostburg? We jumped over the gate, and opened the front door, and... all you have to do is stand still so I can jump off your back and over the gate. On the count of three. One... two—"

Zeph's growl cut her off. "Just because we *can* escape doesn't mean we should. If our people ever found out that we knew how to escape, they'd make it a whole lot harder to do."

"Fine," Sapphie pouted. "But if you're so smart, then how are we going to get that purple thing?"

With that, Sapphie tugged hard on Zeph's ear. Zeph cried before taking hold of the scruff of Sapphie's neck. Before long, the two were barking and running all over the kitchen again. Sapphie jumped on one of the kitchen chairs, knocking down the day's newspaper. As soon as it hit the floor, she tore it to shreds.

~ * ~

The five people in the dining room stopped eating for a minute to listen to the rambunctious puppies.

"Not again," Courtney moaned. "Sapphie, how many times do I have to tell you not to chew up the newspapers?"

Sapphie ran to the kitchen gate and barked victoriously, a scrap of the local section hanging from her mouth. Zeph sat in the corner.

Mrs. Hollinger laughed. "Maybe she's doing us a favor." She turned to Arabella to explain. "You see, my husband doesn't like to get rid of a newspaper until he's read every last word, so they tend to pile up over the week. I guess he won't get to read today's paper."

Arabella frowned and almost looked like she might cry. "That's a shame," Arabella said. "I would have predicted you'd enjoy tonight's paper."

"What do you mean, *you would have predicted*?" Adam asked.

But the puppies barked so loudly that no one heard him.

"It sounds like the puppies are ready to go out," Mr. Hollinger said above the noise.

"I'll let them out," Adam volunteered. He'd do anything to escape having to eat any more asparagus, and to stop Arabella from staring at him.

"I'll come along," Arabella volunteered.

Adam cringed. Why on earth did Arabella want to come along? But then he had an idea. The comic book detective Riley Couth had a Basset hound named Mr. E that he brought with him on cases. When Riley encountered a suspect, he watched the way Mr. E interacted. Mr. E was a good judge of character and could often sniff out a criminal even before Riley found evidence.

Adam remembered how his corgis barked and ran away from Mr. Frostburg. Like Riley Couth's dog, the corgis seemed to be good judges of character. If they ran away from Arabella, it would prove Adam right about distrusting her.

Adam opened the gate and hurried down the stairs of his split-level home, eager to see how the puppies would like their new neighbor.

~ FOUR ~
The Stranger Stranger

In the backyard, Zeph and Sapphie ran circles around Arabella Spinelli. Each time they passed her, Zeph let out a friendly howl, and Sapphie nipped wildly at the air.

"They're so cute," Arabella said.

"Thanks," Adam said.

He tried not to look at her green cat eyes while hiding his disappointment. He rather hoped the dogs would growl at her, but after sniffing for a few minutes, the corgis seemed to like her just fine.

"Hey," she said. "Do you think I can invite my roommate to come over? Her name's Cassandra. She couldn't make it to dinner tonight, but she loves animals. I know she'd just love your dogs."

"I guess so, Miss Spinelli."

"Call me Belle," she said.

Belle flipped open her purple cell phone and sent her roommate a text.

"Not you too," Adam groaned. "My sister has a cell phone just like that. She's always texting."

Belle laughed. "I love texting." A moment later, her cell phone buzzed, and she checked the screen. "Great," she said. "Cassandra's coming over."

"Cassandra?" Adam asked.

"My roommate. We just love this neighborhood. We used to live in an apartment near the college, but it was way too loud. People were always partying. Out here almost feels like we're out in the country. You can just smell all the plants and flowers and herbs growing out here... "

She sat in a lawn chair, and Sapphie jumped onto her lap. "How cute," Belle said. Sapphie's little tail wagged so hard that her entire body trembled, and the pup squealed in excitement. As Belle pet Sapphie, Zeph sat by her feet.

"So, what made you think to check online for the stuff Mister Frostburg stole?" she asked Adam.

"What?" Adam asked. How could she possibly know all these details about the events of this past summer? "I'd rather not talk about all that," he said.

"All right, but I think it was a brave thing for you to do. And smart."

Before Adam's ears had a chance to burn, Cassandra came through the back gate. Adam's eyes popped open wide. If Adam thought Arabella was weird, she was nothing compared to Cassandra.

She seemed to be Arabella's age with silky blonde hair that hung past her waist. She wore bell-bottom jeans and a light green shirt with lots of shiny beads sewn all over it. Her silver bracelets shone with amber jewels, and her fingers, like Arabella's, were decorated with rings, rings, and more rings. But the weirdest thing of all was that she wore a cape. It was velvety black with a hood, though she wasn't wearing the hood.

She had to be the strange figure Adam saw earlier. He took a step backward.

"You must be Adam," Cassandra said, coming toward him. "I'm Cassandra." She flung her cape over her shoulders and cleared her throat. Then she lowered her voice and hunched over, waving her arms like she was casting a spell.

"Fair is foul, and foul is fair," she chanted.

Before Adam could answer, Sapphie jumped
down and sped toward her. Cassandra's cape flut-
tered in the wind, and Zeph shuffled behind a dog-
wood tree. When Sapphie saw Zeph's reaction, she
stopped dead in her tracks and sniffed the air.

"That's odd," Cassandra said. "Animals usually *love* me."

"Sorry," Adam said. "I guess they've never
seen anyone wearing a—"

"A cape," Cassandra finished for him. "I wear
it everywhere now."

"She's a little obsessed," Belle added.

Adam groaned. He'd never seen anyone with a
cape before, except at Halloween. And why were
the corgis so scared? He wondered how Mr. E would
have reacted.

Cassandra crept toward the dogs. She pushed
the cape behind her shoulders and knelt down.
"Here puppies," she called. "It's okay. I'm one of
the good guys."

Sapphie approached first and sniffed Cassandra's extended hand. Cassandra kept stone-still
while Sapphie got closer and closer, her nose sniffing
and sniffing. Finally, Sapphie let out a friendly bark
and gave Cassandra a kiss on the hand.

"That's a good girl," Cassandra said. "What's
her name?"

"Sapphie. It's short for *Princess Sapphire*."

"What a marvelous name," Cassandra said.

Sapphie *definitely* liked that. Without hesita-
tion, she jumped up on Cassandra's knee and bom-
barded her with kisses.

"She sure likes you," Belle said.

"But Zeph doesn't," Adam mumbled.

Zeph was still hiding behind the tree, watching his sister carefully.

"Here boy," Adam called.

Zeph went around the yard the long way to avoid being anywhere near Cassandra. He hid behind Adam with ears back and tiny tail tucked down.

"He looks spooked," Belle said.

"He's usually very friendly," Adam explained. He patted Zeph's head. Then Zeph howled.

"He's just not used to me," Cassandra said. "I'm sure that in time, he'll..." but she couldn't finish her sentence because her cell phone beeped.

"Oh," she said, looking at the screen. "Looks like I forgot about my study session. I've got to run!" She pet Sapphie once more, then dashed out the gate, closing it carefully so that her cape didn't get trapped.

"I've never seen anyone dress like that," Adam said.

"She's trying to get in character," Belle explained.

Adam wasn't sure what Belle meant, but he knew he didn't want anything to do with the two strange young women. Besides, his stomach growled. Three dinner rolls hadn't been enough to fill him up after the disgusting dinner his mother made.

"I have homework," Adam said, hoping he could sneak a peanut-butter sandwich while his mom wasn't looking. As he hurried inside, he nearly slammed into Courtney.

"Watch where you're going, stupid," Courtney said. "And what's your hurry, anyway? Afraid of the boogeyman?" She laughed as Adam hurried inside.

"Courtney," Belle said. "Adam was just telling me that you love to text, just like me."

Courtney smiled as she pulled out her cell phone to compare texting techniques.

~ * ~

In the meantime, Sapphie joined Zeph behind the tree. "I'm going to stay out here and try to get a hold of that purple thing," Sapphie whispered.

"Not me," Zeph whispered back. "I'm going inside with Adam."

"Suit yourself, scaredy-cat," Sapphie said.

"I'm not scared," Zeph said. "It's just that I w-want to spend time with Adam, that's all."

"If you say so," Sapphie said. "But I saw you hiding from those new people."

Zeph didn't answer. He scooted inside as quickly as he possibly could, barely turning to watch as Sapphie crept closer to the purple thing on Bella's head.

~ FIVE ~
Suspicious Young Adults

Adam had never been happier to have math homework to do. It was the perfect excuse to get away from Belle and her weird roommate, Cassandra. With Zeph inside, Adam closed the sliding glass door and drew the curtain. The last thing he needed was for the new neighbors to be looking in on him.

Before Adam went upstairs to work on his homework, he listened to the house. Mr. Hollinger was cleaning up in the kitchen. Courtney was busy outside. His mom was quiet—probably proofreading something for work. Adam finally had the computer to himself. Zeph sat at Adam's feet while Adam logged on to see if any of his friends were online. He wanted someone to talk to about the two strange neighbors.

Luckily, Patrick was logged on, too. Before Adam could even type anything, Patrick sent him a message:

HomeRunPat99: hey adam nice job at practice today!
AdamTheRed: hey patrick thanks, u 2
HomeRunPat99: think well win saturday?
AdamTheRed: hope so
HomeRunPat99: i heard york has a good team.
AdamTheRed: i heard that tooooooo :-(
HomeRunPat99: we can do it
AdamTheRed: :-)
HomeRunPat99: :-)

Just then, Adam heard someone sigh loudly and right behind him. It was a sigh he knew all too well— his mother's. Adam dreaded instant messaging on the computer while his mom was in the room because Mrs. Hollinger was crazy about bad grammar. As a professional copy editor, it was her job to catch all kinds of grammatical and spelling mistakes. Sometimes, she glanced over Adam's homework and cleared her throat every time she caught a spelling error. Other times, she would glance at the computer screen and make sure Adam was using punctuation and capital letters—even when he was messaging his friends.

"Adam Hollinger," she scolded. "How are we supposed to communicate like civilized people when you and your friends insist on typing without even the slightest regard for basic rules of grammar? And don't get me started on your spelling."

"But Mom," Adam complained. "It's just instant messaging. It doesn't count for a grade or anything. Besides, it's so much faster to type without worrying about all that."

"All that?" Mrs. Hollinger asked. "You're talking about the English language, and I just happen to make my livelihood worrying about *all that*. Did you know that in medieval times they didn't even have punctuation?"

"Medieval times?"

"At the rate we're going, we'll be reverting back to a time when people believed in witches," she huffed.

"Witches?" Adam repeated, his eyes wide.

In the meantime, Patrick had sent another message:

HomeRunPat99: R U still there adam?

Mrs. Hollinger took one look at the screen and let out a frustrated yelp. "Is that Patrick?" she asked.

"Yes," Adam groaned.

"Tell him to watch his spelling. And capitalization."

Adam sighed and typed into the computer, being as careful as possible not to make any grammatical mistakes:

AdamTheRed: Patrick, my mom is here.
HomeRunPat99: Hi, Mrs. Hollinger.

Patrick had been friends with Adam long enough to know how much Mrs. Hollinger loved grammar. He knew immediately that he should use capital letters and correct spelling while she was in the room.

"Tell Patrick that he seems much more sophisticated when he uses correct grammar," Mrs. Hollinger said, smiling.

Adam sighed. "Okay, okay, already."

Content, Mrs. Hollinger returned upstairs to help Mr. Hollinger with the rest of the dishes.

Adam started typing again, but he tried to use proper grammar just in case his mom came back.

AdamTheRed: She's gone.
HomeRunPat99: k. i have a lot of homework to do
AdamTheRed: Yeah, I have math 2 do. But can i ask you something first?
HomeRunPat99: u forgot to capitalize your I :-)
AdamTheRed: Can I ask you something?

HomeRunPat99: sure

AdamTheRed: These two weird neighbors just moved into mr. Frostburg's old place.

HomeRunPat99: yeah?

AdamTheRed: one kept staring at me. The other one wears a cape.

HomeRunPat99: a cape?

AdamTheRed: yeah. A real cape. They're creeping me out. But my parents seem to like them. Mom and dad invited one of them for dinner tonight.

HomeRunPat99: what else was weird about them?

AdamTheRed: They had all kinds of weird jewelry. like bracelets and earrings and rings. and one had a weird scarf on her head. like a fortune teller.

HomeRunPat99: antying else?

AdamTheRed: Watch your spelling ;-)

HomeRunPat99: ANYTHING else? :-)

AdamTheRed: Belle is working on something called a Master's degree.

HomeRunPat99: What's she becoming a master of??

AdamTheRed: Not sure. I think Cassandra is going to school, too.

HomeRunPat99: Cassandra? What a name.

AdamTheRed: And the other is named Arabella.

HomeRunPat99: WEIRD. how did the dogs react? didn't you say the dogs didn't like mr frostburg? remember how Mr. E reacts in Riley Couth comics?

AdamTheRed: Already thought of that. Zeph is scared. Sapphie is not.

HomeRunPat99: know what they sound like to me?

AdamTheRed: what?

HomeRunPat99: think Halloween......

AdamTheRed: what about Halloween?

HomeRunPat99: ....witches!!!!

AdamTheRed: witches?

HomeRunPat99: that's what i think. Weird names, weird clothes, weird jewelry... maybe i can come over one day and check them out

AdamTheRed: oh no, i have to rake their leaves for them

HomeRunPat99: perfect

AdamTheRed: how is that perfect?

HomeRunPat99: its the perfect opportunity to spy on them

AdamTheRed: I see. okay, well ask your dad if you can come over one day after practice

HomeRunPat99: okay

AdamTheRed: maybe you could sleep over one night.

HomeRunPat99: k. we'll investigate like detectives. Hey, I hear the new Logan Zephyr comic is about a witch.

AdamTheRed: Really?

HomeRunPat99: Yep. It's called Logan Zephyr and the Space Sorceress. Didn't get a copy yet but I will.

AdamTheRed: Yeah, me too. I have to buy one.

HomeRunPat99: We'll have to read it together. Maybe Logan Zephyr can give us some advice about those neighbors of yours.

AdamTheRed: yeah, we'll have to get a copy. But now it's getting late. We better get our homework done.

HomeRunPat99: yeah. See you at school.

AdamTheRed: k. bye

Just as Adam logged off, Courtney opened the back door and pulled open the curtains. Adam saw Belle waving as she left the backyard. Sapphie scampered in with her ears perked up and her little tail wagging.

"The new neighbors are so cool," Courtney said, smiling.

"Why's that?" Adam asked suspiciously. His sister rarely smiled.

"Did you see Belle's cell phone? It's the coolest thing ever. It has a real camera with night vision. And Belle can text faster than anyone I know."

"Hmph."

"Belle wants to hang out with me some more. With Cassandra."

"That's weird," Adam said.

"What's weird about wanting to hang out with me?"

"Aren't they a little old? They're grownups."

"*Young* grownups," Courtney corrected. "Besides, who wouldn't want to hang out with me? I'm the coolest person ever, remember? Besides, I act old for my age, don't I?"

"If you say so," Adam mumbled.

Courtney frowned. "There's nothing wrong with hanging out with older people. Like Aileen's friend Meghan. She has an older brother who hangs out with us sometimes."

"Hmm," Adam said.

"He's so cool." A dreamy look sparkled in Courtney's eyes. "He's in high school. And he's getting his learner's permit so he can drive, and then he can drive us around and—"

"Mom wouldn't like that."

"Then you'd better not tell her," Courtney threatened.

"Or what?" Even though Adam was usually annoyed at his sister, he still felt protective of her. She didn't always make smart decisions. "A seventh grader hanging out with a tenth grader seems weird."

"If you tell Mom, I'll tell everyone that you have a crush on your teacher *and* on Arabella *and* on Cassandra."

"That's not fair," Adam protested. "Or true."

"Adam and Bella, sitting in a tree, K-I-S-S-I-N-G—" Courtney taunted.

"Fine," Adam said. "I won't tell. Just don't do anything stupid. Be smart for a change."

"Fine," Courtney said.

"I'm going upstairs."

"Good," Courtney said. "'Cause JJ said he'll be online around now to chat with me."

"Who's JJ?"

"JJ is Meghan's older brother, the one who's in high school. Don't you listen to anything I say?"

"The one who's learning how to drive?" Adam asked.

Courtney nodded. "He's so cute. He's even started to grow a beard."

"He sounds way too old for you to be hanging out with."

"And you sound way too much like Mom. Besides, it shows how much you know. You're just a fifth grader."

"Whatever," Adam said.

~ * ~

Adam trudged upstairs but Zeph stayed behind. Sapphie jumped up on the couch, and Zeph followed, looking around to make sure no one had seen. They weren't really supposed to, but Mr. and Mrs. Hollinger were nowhere to be found. Only Courtney was there, and she usually didn't care what they did.

Sapphie wagged her tiny tail. Being on the couch was cool, soft, and fun.

"Sapphie," Zeph whispered. "What did you learn about those two people?"

"What two people?"

Sapphie squirmed, trying to reach a potato chip someone had dropped behind the cushion.

"Sapphie," Zeph growled.

"What already? I'm trying to get a snack, snack, *snack*!"

"Sapphie, tell me about those people you just saw outside."

"Which ones?" Sapphie asked, munching on the chip.

Zeph took a deep breath and remembered his father's words from the day he and Sapphie were adopted. Sapphie had trouble focusing on anything, and Pa Corgi had asked Zeph to keep an eye on her— and to have patience with her, which she pushed to the limits on a daily basis.

"Sapphie," Zeph said as calmly as possible. "You were outside with Courtney and two other people. Remember, one of them had that purple scarf you wanted to chew on?"

"Oh, *those* people," Sapphie remembered.

"Yes, *those* people. Now, what did you learn about them?" Zeph asked.

"For one thing, they wouldn't let me chew on that purple thing."

"Can you blame them?"

"Of course I can! My name isn't just Sapphie. It's *Princess* Sapphie. That means I should be able to do whatever I want. And I wanted to chew, chew, *chew*!"

Zeph sighed again. "Besides not being allowed to chew on the purple thing, what else did you learn about them?"

"Nothing really," Sapphie said. "I was too busy chasing falling leaves. First there was this red one, and it twirled like this... " Sapphie sprang off the couch and spun around to demonstrate.

Zeph growled softly and jumped down to watch. "What about the *people*?"

Sapphie stopped twirling and cocked her head. "Courtney seems to like them."

"I'm worried," Zeph said. "I need you to find out all you can about them."

"Why are you worried?"

"Adam seems afraid of them. And when Adam's worried, then I'm worried."

"You mean *afraid*," Sapphie barked.

"No, not afraid," Zeph said. "Worried."

"That's silly. You should be more like me. I *never* worry. In fact, you know what's almost as good as eating or sleeping? Chewing toys!" With that, she tossed a pink chew toy in the air.

While Sapphie was busy playing, Zeph snuck upstairs to Adam's room, leaving Courtney alone in the glow of the computer screen. Courtney had her back to the room, but as Zeph climbed the stairs, he could see Courtney's face reflected in the computer monitor. He glanced at the mischievous smile curling her lips as her fingers flew across the keyboard, and when he saw the wild gleam in her eye, he hurried upstairs to Adam.

~ SIX ~
Ears on Fire

Adam went to school in a daze. He hadn't slept well. Nightmares haunted him—nightmares of Belle's green cat eyes and black capes that blew mysteriously in the wind. In the classroom, Adam couldn't concentrate, either. When he looked at the clock, all he imagined were the whites of her eyes. When he watched the class's hamster spinning around in its wheel, all he could see were Belle's bangle bracelets. The green graphs on Ms. Wilkerson's chemistry chart only reminded him of the beads Cassandra wore.

And Patrick's words kept echoing through Adam's mind: *Read Logan Zephyr and the Space Sorceress. Maybe your new neighbors are witches...*

Adam was in such a daze, he didn't pay attention when Marnie Ellison sprinkled eraser dust on his chair just before he sat down. He stared into space when the class sang happy birthday to Rudolfo, whose mother brought in cupcakes to celebrate. And he certainly wasn't paying attention when Ms. Paulus told the class that she had a special announcement. In fact, he only snapped out of his daze when he heard his name mentioned in front of the class.

"...and that student," Ms. Paulus was saying, "is Adam Hollinger."

The class applauded. Before Adam realized it, Ms. Paulus was holding up a copy of the local newspaper.

"Why don't you come up here?" Ms. Paulus suggested.

She pointed to the upholstered chair she kept at the front of the room. Normally, students were not allowed in that chair. It was the most comfortable chair in the school, and it was quite an honor to be invited to sit in it. Ms. Paulus used it when she sat in front of the class to read to them, and she allowed special guests to sit in it when they addressed the class. Adam couldn't believe she was inviting him to sit in the chair, and he wished he had been paying a little more attention.

Adam stood, rubbed his eyes, and walked slowly up the aisle. He was concentrating so hard on getting to the chair that he didn't see Marnie Ellison stick her foot right out in front of him. Adam stumbled over her foot. He didn't fall, but he lost his balance and slammed into Gabriella's desk.

"Watch it," Gabriella said.

"Did you have a nice trip?" Tony asked.

"See you next fall," Marnie added.

"Children," Ms. Paulus scolded. She gave Adam a sympathetic look.

Adam could already feel his ears burning. He wondered how red they had turned. It was bad enough that last year the class thought he had a crush on Ms. Wilkerson, his fourth-grade teacher. He hoped Marnie wouldn't try to start that rumor again.

Everyone waited while Adam regained his balance and made it to the front of the room. By the time he sat in the chair, he was too embarrassed to enjoy how comfortable it was. He took a few deep breaths and tried to figure out why in the world Ms. Paulus had called him up there.

Why is she holding a copy of the newspaper?

"Has anyone read last evening's newspaper?" Ms. Paulus asked.

Rudolfo raised his hand. "I read the comics."

"Anyone else?"

No one answered.

"Then you should all go home and read last evening's paper because it features our very own Adam Hollinger."

She held up the front page of the local section. There, front and center, was a picture of Adam and Zeph. It was the picture the reporter took over the summer after Adam helped prove that Mr. Frostburg was the serial burglar. Adam, like his family, assumed the newspaper had decided not to publish the story. But now, weeks later, the story was in print.

"I want to read the article to you," Ms. Paulus told the class. She cleared her throat before reading:

"*This past summer, a local boy and his dog became heroes after solving a string of burglaries that had stumped even local police.*"

Some of Adam's classmates quietly *ooh'd* and *ahh'd*. Adam hadn't told many people about Mr. Frostburg, so only his good friends had heard the story.

"*Local resident Adam Hollinger had seen one too many burglaries this summer and decided to take crime solving into his own hands. When serial burglar James Frostburg made the Hollingers' home his latest target, young Hollinger put his foot down. Hollinger, only ten years old, interviewed neighbors and searched for the stolen goods online, hoping to find a lead to the culprit.*

"'*My parents said the insurance company would help replace the stolen goods, but it couldn't replace my neighbor's heirloom ring, or the neck-*

lace my dad gave to my mom when they first met,'
Adam told us just days after solving the crime. 'I
knew I had to do something to help.'

"Perhaps the only thing more noteworthy
than a ten-year-old solving a crime is his canine
helper. Adam's puppy, a Pembroke Welsh Corgi
named Zeph, had just as much a hand in solving the
crime as Adam. Zeph sniffed out the stolen goods,
was then locked in the shed, and later suffered a
contusion while cornering the suspect.

"Hollinger explains his canine's ability to
help: 'Sometimes I feel like when I talk, Zeph knows
exactly what I'm saying. I know it was probably just
coincidence, but part of me thinks Zeph was pur-
posely looking for our stolen goods in Mr. Frostburg's yard.'

"Frostburg, who was arrested after injuring
the corgi, recently pled guilty to burglary. He re-
ceived a reduced jail sentence, which will be followed by probation and community service.

"One thing can be sure. With Frostburg behind bars, and Adam and Zeph patrolling the neighborhood, residents of Stoney Brook can feel a whole
lot safer."

Ms. Paulus smiled as she finished the article.
"I think we should give Adam a round of applause."

The class applauded, and Adam felt like his
ears were on fire. He looked at all his classmates
clapping for him. Though a small part of him liked
the attention, a larger part of him got nervous
whenever all eyes were on him—like the way he felt
when he pitched at the end of a close game. He
looked at his classmates again and tried to enjoy his
moment in the sun.

Everyone was smiling, clapping, and nodding. Everyone except one—Marnie Ellison had a strange look on her face, as if she was thinking very hard. Adam just knew she had to be plotting some new way to embarrass him, and he only hoped that Marnie would not get Courtney involved.

~ SEVEN ~
Digging for Trouble

While Adam and Courtney were at school, Sapphie and Zeph spent the crisp autumn morning in the back yard. Mr. Hollinger was working in the detached garage out back. A few years ago, he turned the garage into a home office, which he used for his architecture business. If the weather was nice, he let the puppies out before he started work, and he let them back inside at lunchtime. This gave Mrs. Hollinger a chance to concentrate on her copy editing, which she worked on from home.

While both Mr. and Mrs. Hollinger focused on their work, Zeph and Sapphie were left largely unsupervised. As long as they didn't make much noise, they could do as they pleased.

And mischievous little Sapphie took every advantage.

"I've decided how I'm going to apply my digging skills," Sapphie announced.

She had been practicing digging in the garden when her people weren't watching. Digging was one of her favorite things to do—along with sleeping, eating, and chewing. She had been trying for weeks to think of a big digging project that could keep her busy during the mornings.

Zeph growled at his sister. "Sapphie," he said, "we've been over this. Every time you dig, we both get yelled at, and our people fill in the hole."

"I know," Sapphie huffed with a little growl.

"Then why would you continue digging?"

"Digging is the funnest thing in the world! Besides, I already started the project. I started last night when I was out here with Courtney and those two new people."

"You mean Arabella and Cassandra?"

"I don't know *what* their names are, but I'm gonna steal that purple thing, just as soon as I finish digging." Sapphie wagged her stubby tail. "You should've seen me, Zeph. I was digging and digging. Courtney didn't even say a word. She was too busy looking at that shiny, beeping thing."

"You mean her cell phone?"

"Yep. She didn't even notice how much I dug. Want to see it? It's the best hole I've ever made— ever, ever, *ever*!"

Zeph shook his head. He hated doing anything that could get him into trouble. He walked away, plopped down on the patio, and chewed on a rubber toy fire hydrant. He wanted nothing to do with his sister's nefarious plans.

But Sapphie wouldn't be deterred. From the other side of the yard, she lowered her head onto her front paws, leaving her rear end sticking straight up in the air. Zeph could tell she was ready to pounce. He growled a low, rumbling warning, but it had no effect. Sapphie charged her brother, tugging on his ear. He jumped on her, and before long, they were tumbling across the lawn.

After struggling and struggling, Sapphie pinned Zeph on his back.

"Will you listen to my plan now?" she asked.

Zeph knew from past experience that when Sapphie wanted something, she wouldn't stop pestering him until she got it.

"Fine," Zeph said. "Just get off me."

Sapphie sprang up and sat at attention.

Zeph rolled over and slowly rose to his feet, cleaning off crumbled leaves from his paws. "Fine," he sighed. "What's your plan?"

"See that big, smelly pile over there?" Sapphie pointed with her nose to the Hollingers' compost pile.

"We're not supposed to go over there," Zeph reminded her. "Adam told me so. And the one time you jumped onto that pile, Courtney smacked you with a rolled-up newspaper."

"Hmph," Sapphie snorted. "Haven't you learned yet that following the rules is boring?"

Zeph sighed. "What does the compost pile have to do with digging? If you dig in there, Courtney will surely give you a..." Zeph didn't finish his sentence.

"A what, Zeph?" Sapphie asked.

"I don't even want to say it."

"What are you talking about? What will Courtney give me if I dig in the compost pile?"

"Remember what happened last time?"

"A bath?" Sapphie asked.

As soon as she said it, both puppies began to tremble. They'd only ever had two baths before, and it wasn't any fun. Zeph had been especially afraid of the water. Sapphie loved the water, but she hated the shampoo. She tried to bite all the tiny bubbles, and she cried wildly as soon as Courtney squirted the smelly shampoo on her coat.

"I don't ever want another one of those," Sapphie whispered, still trembling.

"Neither do I."

The pair stayed silent for a moment while they tried to think of something happy. In the meantime, Mr. Hollinger emerged from his office and peered over the fence.

"You dogs okay?" he asked. "You were so quiet, I thought you'd run off somewhere."

He came to the edge of the fence and bent down. "You two look like you've seen a ghost."

Both puppies ran toward him, happy that the distraction made them forget all about having a bath.

After petting both dogs, Mr. Hollinger stood. "I'm going to meet a client," he told them. "You two be good while I'm gone. Pretty soon, Susan will let you inside for lunch."

Sapphie barked at the mention of lunch. It was a human word even Sapphie knew. The puppies sat at attention while watching Mr. Hollinger get into his car and drive away.

"I sure wish we were going for a ride in the car," Zeph said.

"Why?" asked Sapphie.

"Don't you remember the times we went for a ride in the car? It's so fun to stick your head out the window and sniff all the air passing by," Zeph remembered.

"Not as fun as being left home alone while somebody *else* goes away in the car!" A mischievous sparkle gleamed in her eye.

"What are you talking about?" Zeph asked.

"Mom is always busy inside reading all those papers," Sapphie explained.

"So?"

"So now Dad is leaving."

"So?"

"Zeph, come on! With both of them out of our fur, we have the yard to ourselves. We can do whatever we want."

"All I want to do is sit here, chew on this toy, and hope that Adam comes home soon."

"He won't be back for a while. Ever since this *school* thing started, Adam and Courtney are gone all day."

"I don't like it. Remember when we first moved here? Adam and Courtney were home almost all the time."

Without warning, Sapphie barked loudly right in Zeph's face.

"What was that for?" Zeph asked.

"You're taking up too much time."

"Time for what?"

"Digging, digging, *digging*!"

Sapphie ran behind the compost pile. Zeph could already hear her claws scratching the rough soil.

Zeph took a quick look at the house to make sure Mrs. Hollinger wasn't watching. He didn't see her, so he snuck behind the compost pile with Sapphie.

The compost pile was the most interesting smelling thing in the Hollingers' yard. Usually it just smelled like fresh grass clippings or decomposing leaves. But every once in a while the Hollingers mixed in some egg shells, old vegetables, or fruit, and Zeph couldn't help but take a long whiff of a decomposing watermelon rind.

"Zeph, over here," Sapphie whispered.

Zeph moved to the very back corner of the yard. There were about six inches of space between the edge of the compost pile and the edge of the fence. Sapphie had squeezed her way into this space and was frantically digging under the fence.

"I'm almost there," she said. "Want to help?"

"Sapphie," Zeph warned, his eyes bulging. "Are you digging an escape hole?"

"*Escape* sounds so harsh," Sapphie said. "Think of it more as an *adventure tunnel*."

Zeph growled. "And what are you going to do when you get out of the yard?"

"Try to find that purple thing Arabella was wearing. I can't wait to chew it, chew it, *chew it*! Last night, she wouldn't let me near it. But I'll get my teeth on it yet."

"I'm not sure I like the idea of escaping."

Sapphie pouted. "But it worked this summer," Sapphie reminded him. "By escaping, we were actually able to *help* our People. Remember?"

Zeph cocked his head. Then he walked to the other side of the compost heap while Sapphie resumed her work.

"Where are you going, chicken? Too scared to help?" Sapphie panted while she dug.

"No," Zeph said. "I can't believe I'm saying this, but you're right. Escaping *did* help last summer, so I'll keep watch. If I give three barks, it means one of our people is nearby."

With that, Sapphie gave a grateful bark and quickened her pace as she dug with all her might.

~ EIGHT ~
Lunchtime Shake-Up

At lunch, everyone wanted to sit next to Adam. When the class lined up to walk to the cafeteria, Ms. Paulus let Adam move to the front and lead. When the class arrived at the cafeteria, everyone followed Adam to the two tables assigned to Ms. Paulus' class. Adam wasn't good friends with many people in his homeroom, so he usually just sat wherever there was an open seat. But today, no one sat down until Adam had chosen a seat on the end of the second table.

"Mind if I sit here?" Olivia asked, scooting in next to Adam.

"I guess not," Adam said. Olivia usually didn't give him the time of day.

"I get to sit on the other side of Adam," Amira called out. She sat on the end and slid over, pushing Adam and Olivia further down the bench.

Melanie and Priya sat directly across from Adam.

"Hi Adam," both said in cheerful unison.

Adam nodded as he opened his lunch. He hoped his ears didn't turn red. He had never been surrounded by girls in the lunchroom before.

"I think it's really brave that you helped to stop that robber," Olivia said.

"It was a burglar, not a robber, right Adam?" Amira asked.

"Yeah, tell us about it," Melanie said excitedly.

Adam looked up to see Marnie Ellison standing on the other side of the table, staring at him. Her eyebrows were drawn together in a scowl, and she took the last remaining seat all the way at the other end of the table. In her hand was a can of soda Adam had seen her shaking on the way to the cafeteria. She glared at Adam's corner of the table before she opened her lunch and ate in a hurry.

"Come on, Adam," Olivia said. "Tell us about your summer."

Adam turned away from Marnie and told them about his experiences with the burglary and baseball and the puppies. He skipped a lot of the details because he wasn't used to such attention.

"So, Adam," Olivia said after Adam recounted his adventures. "Are you going to the Harvest Dance?"

"Um... " Adam's ears felt as if they were about to catch fire, and he took a few deep breaths.

The Harvest Dance was for the fourth and fifth graders at Stoney Brook Elementary. Since the dance was held near Halloween, most students went in costume, and there was a costume contest. At the beginning of the dance, the first, second, and third graders were allowed to come and join the Pumpkin Parade around the outside of the school and inside the school gym. Then, everyone gathered in the auditorium where the judges announced the winners. Afterward, the younger kids went home, but the older kids could go to the dance in the gym.

"Yeah, Adam," Amira said. "Are you going to the Harvest Dance?"

"Are you bringing anyone as your date?" Melanie asked.

Now Adam's ears felt *really* red. Usually everyone just went with a group of friends, and only a handful of fifth graders brought someone as a date.

"We could go together as matching cartoon characters," Melanie suggested.

"Or you could go as a police detective and I could go as a cat burglar," Priya offered.

Adam looked up briefly to see Marnie glaring, shooting daggers at him.

"I'm really not sure if I'm going," Adam said. "The dance is the same night as the last game of Autumn League playoffs. So I might be away. If my team makes it that far," he added.

"You're on Autumn League?" Melanie asked. "That's so cool."

"I think it's cool, too," Olivia swooned.

"So," Priya said. "If you *do* get to go to the dance, would you like to go together?"

All four pairs of eyes stared expectantly at Adam.

"Um," he stuttered, stalling for time.

Up until today, he hadn't been good friends with any of them, and now they were all asking him to go to the dance with them. He didn't know what to say.

Behind him, Marnie Ellison huffed. Even though students weren't allowed to get up and walk around, Marnie had risked it. She shook up her unopened soda can one more time and crinkled up her trash. She went to the trash can and made a detour on the way back to her seat, looking over her shoulder to make sure the lunch monitors weren't watching.

"Here, Adam," she said. "I'm too full to drink my soda. I figured since you're a disgusting boy, you'll drink anything. So you can have it."

Behind her back, a lunch monitor cleared his throat. "Back to your seat," he told Marnie.

"Sorry," she said in her sweetest voice ever. "I was just giving this soda to my friend."

"No sharing food," the lunch monitor said, eyeing both Adam and Marnie. "Go back to your seat."

Marnie scowled and went back to her seat with the soda still in her hand.

After the lunch monitor moved on to a new table, Chad turned to Marnie. "I'll have that soda if you don't want it," he whispered, and grabbed the soda from her.

Marnie tried to stop him, but it was too late. Before she could say anything, Chad popped the top open. The children at the table screamed with laughter as the shaken soda exploded into a fizzy fountain and drenched Chad. Two lunch monitors ran over with a stack of napkins, and the rest of the class stood on benches to watch. Adam was glad for the distraction because he didn't have to answer any of the four girls about the Harvest Dance.

Marnie Ellison was late returning from lunch. She entered the class red-faced with a pass from the principal, and Ms. Paulus made her apologize to Chad before taking her seat. She walked down the aisle to her seat and glared at Adam, leaving his skin prickling the rest of the day.

~ NINE ~
The Scariest Word in the English Language

Finally, after what seemed like endless digging, Sapphie was finished. She had dug a small hole under the fence.

"What do you think, Zeph?" she asked.

Zeph craned his neck around the compost heap. He had been keeping an eye out for Mrs. Hollinger and didn't want to abandon his post.

"Are you sure you can squeeze through there?" he asked.

"Yes. Duh! Are you calling me *fat*?" she asked.

"No," Zeph said. "But both of us are getting bigger every day. Haven't you noticed?"

"Hmph," Sapphie scowled. "I can fit through just fine. You want to see?"

Before Zeph could answer, he heard the back door open. Out stepped Mrs. Hollinger.

"Zeph," she called. "Sapphie, come in for lunch."

Zeph came running, followed by Sapphie. But the look on Mrs. Hollinger's face told Zeph there was a problem.

"Sapphie, what did you get into this time?"

Sapphie's paws, which were normally white like socks, were now covered in dirt.

"Were you digging a hole?" Mrs. Hollinger walked around the yard in slow circles, searching the ground for signs of digging.

"Zeph, what'll we do?" Sapphie squealed. "If she finds my hole, she'll never let me keep it."

Zeph watched Mrs. Hollinger for a minute. "I don't believe I'm about to do this," he said.

"Do what?" Sapphie asked.

But Zeph didn't have time to answer. Before Sapphie knew what was happening, Zeph ran to the other side of the yard and started frantically digging a hole.

"Not you too, Zeph," Mrs. Hollinger scolded. "I thought only Sapphie liked to dig."

She chased Zeph away from the hole and he yelped. Zeph hated disobeying the rules and being scolded.

Sapphie, meanwhile, was so delighted that Zeph had started digging that she joined in. She jumped into the hole Zeph started and dug some more.

"Dig, dig, *dig!*" she barked.

"That's it," Mrs. Hollinger said. "You two are getting a bath."

Both dogs froze in terror, dropping low on the ground.

"That's right. You're covered in mud, and I won't have you tracking it through the house. Now stay right here while I get the towels. I'm going to be far behind on my editing after this little delay. I hope you two are happy with yourselves."

Zeph and Sapphie cowered at her feet.

"Stay," she commanded. Then she disappeared into the house.

"Zeph, why did you do that?" Sapphie asked when Mrs. Hollinger was out of sight. She was trembling.

"I didn't want her filling in your hole," Zeph said, also shaking.

"Why, Zeph, I didn't think you were any fun at all."

"The hole might come in handy," he explained. "I've still got a strange feeling about this Arabella person. She scares Adam, and that scares me."

"I have a strange feeling, too," Sapphie said. "A strange feeling that I'm going to chew up that purple scarf, scarf, *scarf*!"

But Mrs. Hollinger emerged, ruining Sapphie's jolly thought. The dogs rolled onto their backs, allowing Mrs. Hollinger to wrap them in towels and carry them off to the horrors of the bathtub upstairs.

~ * ~

After Mrs. Hollinger finished washing the dogs, she brought them into the kitchen and gave them lunch. While they were eating, she glanced at the clock and tapped her nails.

"Your digging has made me late," she told the dogs.

Zeph ran up to her, sat at attention, and howled once. Mrs. Hollinger couldn't help but smile.

"You're cute," she told them. "But you're mischievous. Let's go back outside and see if Doug is back from his meeting yet. If he is, I'll let you stay outside again, but *no digging*," she said firmly.

Both puppies sat at attention while she scribbled something on a pad and left it on the kitchen table. Then, the puppies obediently followed her outside. Mrs. Hollinger left through the fence gate and disappeared into the converted garage.

"You got us in trouble," Zeph said.

"Not my fault," Sapphie insisted. "You could have stayed out of trouble. *I* never told you to dig. That was your decision. I still don't get why you did it."

"I told you," Zeph said. "Our escape hole—or *adventure tunnel*, as you call it—might be useful. But we've got to agree on something important." Zeph turned to watch Mrs. Hollinger get into her car and wave.

"Doug is in his office," she said through the car's open window. "He'll keep an eye on you two, so *no digging*."

"We have to agree," Zeph continued, still facing the driveway as Mrs. Hollinger drove away, "that we won't use that hole to escape unless it is an absolute emergency."

With that, he turned to face his sister but he was too late. She had already disappeared behind the compost pile and into the hole. Zeph ran over just in time to see her stubby little tail disappear, and then emerge on the other side of the fence.

Sapphie didn't look back. Instead, she ran as fast as her little legs could take her—straight to Arabella Spinelli's house.

~ TEN ~
For the Love of a Scarf

Courtney came home while Adam went to practice. As she walked home from the bus stop, she kept checking her cell phone. She couldn't even focus on the music playing in her ear buds—she just wanted her cell phone to beep. JJ had promised to text her after school, and she couldn't wait. He said he wanted to make Halloween plans with Courtney, Aileen, and Meghan. He was already in tenth grade, and Courtney was sure he would think of something fun to do for Halloween.

JJ still hadn't sent her a text by the time she got home, so she went into the kitchen for a snack. There, on the kitchen table, she saw a hastily-scrawled note from her mom—written with perfect grammar, of course.

Dear Courtney,

The dogs got into some mud in the backyard, so I had to give them a bath. Because of the bath, I was running late, so I had to run some errands this afternoon and drop off some copy editing work I've completed.

Please check on the dogs when you get home. I asked Dad to look after them, but you know how he gets so wrapped up in his work. Please make sure they aren't digging in the yard again.

Oh, Adam has practice again today. It would be really nice of you if you walked both Sapphie and Zeph. I'm sure Zeph has been feeling lonely with Adam being gone so late at practice these past weeks.

Thanks, and I'll see you soon.

Love, Mom

Courtney left the note on the table and went to the back window to check on the dogs. She saw Zeph lying on the patio chewing on a toy. She didn't see Sapphie but figured she must be somewhere. Courtney shrugged, checked her cell phone again, and returned to the kitchen for a snack.

She grabbed a package of cinnamon graham crackers, poured a glass of milk, and went upstairs to her room. Even though no one else was home, she closed her door and plugged her mp3 player into her speakers. Then she opened one of her magazines and settled onto her pillow to read.

~ * ~

Coach Harris drove both Patrick and Adam to Adam's house after practice. Patrick was staying for dinner because he wanted to get a look at the two new neighbors to see if they really were witches. When the boys entered Adam's house, the sky had already begun to darken, but no lights were on inside.

"That's funny," Adam said. "Mom's usually home by now."

He and Patrick took off their muddy cleats in the entryway and walked up to the kitchen. There was no sign of dog or person.

"Where is everybody?" Patrick asked.

"I'm not sure." Adam saw the note his mother had left on the kitchen table. "Maybe Courtney's actually walking the puppies," Adam said after reading it.

"Doesn't sound like it," Patrick said. He pointed up the stairs. Adam craned his neck around the doorway and heard Courtney's music spilling into the hallway.

"She must be locked up in her room again," Adam said. "All she ever wants to do now is spend time in her room with the door closed and the music playing. And she usually has Sapphie in there with her. I sure hope Zeph isn't stuck in there with those two."

"Where else would he be?"

"Let's look outside," Adam suggested.

When the two boys went into the backyard, Zeph greeted them with an excited howl.

"Hey, Zeph," Adam said. Zeph turned over so Adam could rub his belly. "You all by yourself, boy?"

Zeph flipped over and barked twice.

"Where's Sapphie?" Adam asked. "Is she upstairs with Courtney?"

Zeph barked again.

"Shh," Adam said. But Zeph wouldn't stop barking.

"Maybe a walk will calm him down," Patrick suggested. He smiled mischievously. "Besides, maybe we can get a glimpse of these two weirdos you were telling me about."

"Okay," Adam said. "I'm telling you, they're the weirdest people I've ever met."

Zeph sat at attention at the mention of a *walk*. Patrick bent down to pet Zeph while Adam went inside for a leash. A moment later, the three of them headed down the street.

"So I read that article about you in the paper last night," Patrick said.

"You and everybody else," Adam muttered. "The librarians at school saved me three copies."

"You should be proud of being famous," Patrick told him. "I heard that Ms. Paulus made a big deal out of it in front of your class. I also heard that Marnie Ellison tripped you in front of everyone."

Adam's ears heated as he remembered the embarrassing incident. "Where did you hear that?" Patrick was in Ms. Wilkerson's class—news traveled fast at Stoney Brook Elementary.

"Marnie texted Tyra right before lunch, and Tyra told our whole class while we were eating."

Adam shook his head and felt his face flush. "She didn't trip me... she just made me stumble a little. I don't understand why she's always picking on me. I try to ignore her."

Patrick couldn't help but laugh. "Maybe you should try paying attention to her," he suggested.

"Pay attention to her? Why?"

"I overheard Tyra telling her friends the reason Marnie torments you is... No, never mind. I shouldn't say anything."

Adam stopped short. "Come on, Patrick. You can't just stop right in the middle of telling me something important. Tell me!"

Patrick tried not to laugh. "Tyra was saying the reason Marnie torments you is..." he sighed. "She has a crush on you."

Adam pulled his Lancaster Reds cap down low, trying to hide his burning ears. He made a sound halfway between a grunt and the beginning of a sentence but stopped himself.

The two boys walked in silence for a few minutes. As they got closer to Arabella's house, Zeph pulled frantically against his leash. Adam was glad for the distraction. He didn't want to tell Patrick about the girls and the Harvest Dance.

"Calm down, Zeph," Adam said, hoping that Patrick would forget about the article and Tyra. And especially, Marnie Ellison.

But it didn't work. Even with Zeph as a distraction, Patrick brought up what Adam hoped he wouldn't.

"After school, Marnie told me you had a line of girls asking to go to the Harvest Dance with you."

Adam felt his face heating again. He wondered if it was as red as his baseball cap. "It wasn't like that," he said, looking at the ground.

Patrick laughed. "Still, only a few fifth graders get to bring a date to the dance."

"Yeah, because only a few actually want to. Those girls are a pain. They want to dress up in matching costumes. Who wants to deal with all that?"

Patrick laughed. "Hopefully, we'll still be in the playoffs then, and if we win our final game, you'll be too busy celebrating with the team to worry about the dance."

Before Adam could answer, Zeph barked and started to pull Adam up Arabella's driveway.

"No, Zeph," Adam called. For a little dog, Zeph was very strong.

Adam tried to pull Zeph away until Belle's front door opened and out she stepped. Adam had to rub his eyes. He couldn't believe what he saw. In Belle's arms was Sapphie—with a purple scarf tied in a bow around her neck!

~ ELEVEN ~
Into the Cauldron

"This is that weird lady I was telling you about," Adam whispered to Patrick.

"She definitely looks like a witch to me," Patrick said as softly as he could under Zeph's frantic barking.

Sapphie looked as calm as could be. Her purple scarf matched Belle's purple skirt. Belle also wore strange sandals that looked like they belonged on a Roman gladiator. She had just as many bangle bracelets as the last time Adam saw her, and now she tied her long hair back with a bright yellow bandana.

"Maybe you're right," Adam said. "How else would she have got a hold of Sapphie?"

Before Patrick could answer, Arabella called down the driveway. "I just made a fresh batch of warm, mulled cider. Would you boys like some?"

Patrick turned to Adam. "No way," he said. "She might be a witch, and it might be a poisoned brew."

"But if we have apple cider with her, maybe we can gather evidence," Adam said.

"That's true," Patrick whispered. "Riley Couth would tell us to go investigate. You know—gather evidence."

Adam grunted. "Okay, but if she turns us into toads, you owe me one."

Patrick laughed nervously.

Zeph pulled Adam up the slanted driveway. When they got to the front porch, Belle put Sapphie on the ground beside Zeph. Immediately, Zeph quieted and sniffed his sister intently.

"How did you get a hold of Sapphie?" Adam asked, trying his best to hide his suspicion.

"She must have gotten loose," Belle said. "Come inside. The cider's nice and hot."

Adam gave Patrick a questioning glance before following Belle inside. Even when Mr. Frostburg had lived in the house, Adam had never been inside. He wasn't sure what to expect.

As soon as they entered the doorway, they followed Belle down three steps into the family room. The whole place smelled like autumn—a mix of cinnamon and vanilla, pumpkin spice and apple.

"It smells like the cider's just about ready," Belle said. "Have a seat. Make yourselves at home. Actually, if one of you wants to come up here and help me carry some cider?"

"Sure thing," Patrick volunteered.

He gave Adam a nervous glance before following her into the kitchen. Adam peered through the kitchen doorway to see a large kettle bubbling on the stove. *It's like a witch's cauldron,* he thought while watching Belle ladle a spoonful of the bubbling liquid into a clear mug and hand it to Patrick.

He turned away and took Zeph off his leash, looking around the strange room. There was a small television in the corner, and a couch covered in a purple tapestry with black stars and yellow moons. On the other side of the room was a small, round table with two folding chairs. The table was covered in a Halloween-themed tablecloth with dancing skeletons, jack-o-lanterns, and witches. Spread on top of it was a deck of very large cards.

The rest of the room was a mystery. There were pieces of furniture, or maybe boxes, all covered in various tapestries, some plain colors, and others decorated with Celtic knots, dragons, or fairies. Adam couldn't tell what was underneath them.

When Belle and Patrick returned carrying three mugs of hot apple cider, Belle handed one to Adam. He sat on the couch and took a sip, finding, to his surprise, it tasted delicious. Even Patrick would have to admit that it didn't taste like witch's brew. The three of them sat on the couch sipping cider while Sapphie and Zeph lay in the corner behind one of the tapestry-covered mysteries.

The décor of the house was so strange that for a moment, Adam forgot to ask how Sapphie ended up there.

"You sure have a lot of tapestries," Adam commented.

"Oh, they're just covering all of our boxes," Belle said. "Cassie and I haven't had a chance to fully unpack yet. I've been busy with my schoolwork, and Cassie's been busy with her job and hobbies. She's opening a new daycare facility in town, and she's been busy painting murals on all the walls before she opens. She's quite an artist. Not to mention actress."

Adam nodded.

"What's this?" Patrick asked, pointing at the strange cards on the little table.

"They're tarot cards," Belle said. "You're supposed to use them to tell fortunes."

Adam and Patrick exchanged glances. *See, she is a witch*, Patrick's eyes seemed to shout.

"Whose fortune were you telling?" Patrick asked.

Belle laughed. "Actually," she said, "I was telling Sapphie's."

"You were reading a dog's fortune?"

Belle smiled. "Yes."

"So what does her future hold?" Adam asked.

"According to the cards, Sapphie is quite a troublemaker, though she has a good heart."

"You got that right," Adam said. "Anything else?"

"That's as far as I got. I had her sitting in one of the chairs," Belle said, blushing.

Adam looked at Patrick and rolled his eyes.

"But then she jumped down and started barking. I looked out the window, and that's when I saw you two and Zeph."

"That reminds me," Adam said. "You never did tell us how Sapphie ended up in your house... and wearing a purple scarf."

Belle smiled. "I think purple looks very becoming on her. Very regal and elegant."

Again, Adam rolled his eyes.

Belle continued. "I was inside doing my schoolwork when I heard scratching on the back door, and there was little Sapphie, all by herself. I let her inside, and when I sat down on the couch to call your parents, she jumped up on me and got a hold of my scarf. She just wouldn't let go. So I let her keep it. It looks nice on her, don't you think?"

Adam groaned. He thought it was dumb to dress up pets. It was something only a girl would think of doing. "Why didn't you bring her back to our house?" Adam asked.

"I tried," Belle insisted. "No one answered the phone. I rang the doorbell, but no one answered. I knocked, and nothing. I even went into the back yard. Zeph was sleeping on the patio, and I didn't want to upset him, so I came back here. I figured someone would come home sooner or later."

Belle looked at the boys' clothing. "You two look like you just came back from baseball practice."

"Yeah," Adam said. "Patrick's on the team, too. His dad is the coach."

"Nice to meet you, Patrick. I'm Arabella. Belle for short." Belle held out her hand, and Patrick paid careful attention to all the weird rings and bracelets she wore.

"It's strange that no one answered the door," Patrick said as he shook her hand. "Adam's sister was home. Courtney."

"That's odd," said Belle.

"No it's not." Adam sighed. "My sister plays the music so loud in her room she probably wouldn't hear an earthquake. If you ever need to contact her, you might as well just text her. My mom left a note for her to walk both dogs when she got home, but it looks like she just went right up to her room instead. She's been like that recently. Wants to spend all her time up there. Her stupid friend has this stupid brother who's in high school already. Courtney's practically obsessed with him."

"That doesn't sound right," Belle said. "I mean, Courtney's only in seventh grade, right? She shouldn't be hanging around with high school students. Do your parents approve?"

"They don't even know," Adam said. "She does everything through her phone with text messages, and my parents think she's just texting with Aileen and her other friends. They'd probably flip out if they knew."

"Maybe you should tell them, Adam," Patrick said. "You know, to get back at Courtney for all the times she's been a pain in your neck."

Adam considered it. "Maybe."

"Maybe you *should* tell on her," Belle said, sipping her cider.

"I don't want to be a tattle-tale," Adam sighed. "Especially because Courtney likes to start rumors about me with her friends, and Marnie always joins in."

Belle frowned. "Maybe you should let me talk to her instead," Belle suggested. "We had a nice, long talk last night, and I feel as if I know her like a best friend. Sometimes girls her age would rather listen to someone like me instead of her parents. Maybe I should text her more often?"

Adam shook his head. "I don't understand her. I always listen to my parents."

Patrick laughed. "Yeah, Adam, but not everyone is a goody-goody like you."

"Well," Adam said, feeling his ears burn, "I should get back. Mom will probably be home soon."

"So soon?" Belle asked. "You didn't even finish your cider. It's good for you. You should finish it."

Adam exchanged glances with Patrick. Why was it so important for him to finish his cider? Maybe it really *was* a potion.

"Maybe another sip," Adam said. "But I'm sure my mom's waiting with dinner."

Belle peered out the window. "Actually, it doesn't look like she's home yet. Her car's not in your driveway."

"Hmm," Adam grumbled, feeling trapped. He just wanted to get home, but none of his excuses were working. He took a deep breath and gulped down the rest of the cider. "That was good," he said abruptly. "Thanks for the cider, and thanks for watching Sapphie."

"It wasn't any trouble at all. It was a pleasure, in fact." As Belle spoke, she looked right into Adam's eyes again. He felt a shudder travel down his spine. "Oh, and Adam?" she asked.

"Yes?"

"Do you think you'll be able to rake some leaves soon? It's an absolute mess back there."

"I guess... I'm pretty busy with practice right now though."

"Tomorrow's a light practice, Adam," Patrick said. "We have a game on Saturday, remember?"

"Great," Belle said. "Then it's settled. You can come over tomorrow."

"Thanks, Patrick," Adam muttered under his breath. He'd hoped to use baseball practice as an excuse to avoid the creepy house where Mr. Frostburg used to live—and the strange new residents.

"I'd sure be interested in having my fortune read sometime," Patrick said to Belle, looking at the cards on the table.

Belle smiled. "Anytime," she said. "In fact, if you wanted to come over while Adam's raking leaves, I'd be happy to read your cards for you."

"I'll ask my dad," Patrick said.

"That's a great idea," Adam said sarcastically and bent over to put Zeph's leash back on. "We've got to get back now," he told Arabella.

As they left, Patrick took hold of Zeph's leash, and Adam carried Sapphie.

"Why did you agree to get your fortune read by her?" Adam asked when they were well down the street and out of earshot.

"She might be a real witch. But the only way to find out for sure is to do more investigating. You said yourself that she was right about Sapphie being a troublemaker. Maybe she really can read fortunes. Besides, think about what Riley Couth would do."

"That's true," Adam said, remembering his favorite comic book detective. "He'd want us to gather as much evidence as we can."

"Besides, I didn't get to meet the other one. What was her name?"

"Cassandra," Adam said. "Cassie."

"Is she the one that wears the cape?"

Adam nodded.

"Sweet. I can't wait to meet her. I'll bet *she's* the head witch." Patrick grinned. "So is it okay if I go over there tomorrow while you're raking leaves?" Patrick asked.

Adam had a stern look on his face. "It's better than me going there by myself. This way if she is a witch, we'll have a chance against her. Two to one is pretty good odds. And when you're done getting your fortune read, if she hasn't turned you into a toad, you can help me rake leaves."

Patrick laughed.

"But right now," Adam said, "I've got something more important to deal with."

"What's that?" Patrick asked.

"Courtney," Adam said with a huff and a scowl.

~ Twelve ~
Three Times for Trouble

Adam put the dogs in the kitchen, closed the safety gate, and scowled. The dogs sat quietly and watched him trudge up the stairs. Patrick patted them each on the head and followed Adam.

"Sapphie," Zeph scolded. "I was so worried about you. Where were you?"

"I *told* you already," Sapphie said, lying down on the comforter. "I really wanted this purple scarf. I was going to chew it up, but that nice lady said it looks pretty on me. Don't you think so?"

Sapphie posed, modeling the scarf for her brother. Zeph growled.

"She said it looks *regal*. What does that mean?" Sapphie asked.

"It means it looks like something a princess might wear."

Sapphie wagged her tail. "It's because I *am* a princess. Princess Sapphie is my name," she cheered, running around in circles. "Princess, princess, *princess!*"

"Why were you gone so long?" Zeph growled.

"Arabella tried to bring me back," Sapphie explained after she calmed down. "But no one answered the door. How come you didn't hear the doorbell?"

"I was all the way out back," Zeph said.

"So see, it's just as much your fault as it is mine."

"No, it's not," Zeph said, plopping down on the floor.

"It is too," Sapphie insisted, prancing in a wide circle around Zeph. "Besides, I succeeded in getting the scarf."

"That scarf isn't important," Zeph said.

Sapphie charged him and pulled his ear. "Take it back," she threatened. "This scarf is *too* important. Just look how it compliments my eyes."

Zeph growled and rolled away from his sister. "Besides, I think you got Courtney in trouble," Zeph said. "Did you see how mad Adam was? I've never seen him that mad. I'm sure glad he left us in the kitchen."

"Why?"

"I wouldn't want to hear the fighting going on between him and Courtney."

"Fighting?" Sapphie jumped up from her comforter. "I want to hear, hear, *hear!*" She ran to the safety gate and perked up her ears.

"Sapphie, we have more important things to discuss," Zeph said.

"Shhh. I can't hear."

"Sapphie," Zeph barked.

"What?"

"I need to ask you some questions about Arabella. She's making Adam rake leaves for her tomorrow. I plan on coming along, and I need to be prepared. Now this is important—Patrick and Adam seem to think Arabella is... well, a witch."

"What's a witch?" Sapphie asked.

"I don't know," Zeph admitted. "But it doesn't sound good." Zeph was the smartest of his brothers and sisters, and he knew most words that people used in daily conversation. But he had never heard the word *witch* until today.

"Maybe Mister Frostburg was a witch?" Sapphie suggested.

"Maybe you're right," Zeph agreed. "And he was a bad man. He stole our People's things, and he hurt my leg."

"Maybe anyone who lives in that spooky old house is just automatically a witch?" Sapphie licked one paw.

"That makes sense," Zeph said. "Now I'm worried."

"Well, don't worry, you worry-wart. Arabella is nothing like Mister Frostburg. Didn't you see the pretty scarf she gave me? Maybe she's a *good* witch."

Zeph rolled his eyes. "Did she say anything about turning you into a toad?"

"A toad?" Sapphie asked. "Are you serious? I thought you were smart, Zeph. How could she turn me into a toad? Where would you get that idea?"

Zeph plopped to the ground in frustration. "Oh, just something I heard Adam mention."

"I plan to go back tomorrow."

"Tomorrow?"

"Arabella let me sit in this really comfy chair, and she was playing with these weird cards. I couldn't understand what she was saying, but I sure enjoyed the attention."

"No, Sapphie," Zeph insisted. "You can't go back there. Not tomorrow. Not ever. That hole you dug was a bad idea. It's only supposed to be used in emergencies, but you're already using it way too much."

"Nonsense," Sapphie said. "I'll never get caught. I'm much too cute to get caught."

Zeph growled. "When I go to Arabella's tomorrow, I want you to stay here. And while I'm gone, you listen carefully. If I bark three times, that means I'm in trouble. If you hear me bark three times, I want you to use your escape tunnel to get loose and try to help me."

"Oh, so now you *want* me to use my tunnel. What's it worth to you?" Sapphie asked.

"Come on, Sapphie. I would do the same for you."

"But I'm not you," she huffed. "What's it worth to you?" she asked again.

"I'll give you my cookie tonight," Zeph said.

"It's a deal."

"So how many times will I bark if I'm in trouble?"

"Two." Sapphie said.

Zeph growled.

"Just kidding," Sapphie said. "Three. Three times for trouble."

Just as Sapphie jumped up to bite her brother's ear, the puppies heard Mr. Hollinger's heavy footsteps coming up the stairs, and they both ran excitedly to the safety gate, forgetting for a moment about the mysterious Arabella Spinelli or the possible fight taking place upstairs.

~ THIRTEEN ~
The Upper Hand

Adam headed up the stairway toward Courtney's room. Adam looked pretty mad, and Patrick followed eagerly behind.

"Are you finally going to get Courtney in trouble?" Patrick asked as they approached Courtney's door.

"I don't know yet," Adam said. "I need to talk to her first."

When they got to her door, Adam opened it without even knocking. She was reclining at her desk—leaning back on the two back legs of her chair. Her music was blasting, and she was typing a text message on her cell phone.

"Courtney," Adam yelled.

Courtney didn't respond, so Adam turned down her music.

Courtney spun around with a wild look in her eye. "Hey! Who said you could come in? Get out, stupid!" she screamed.

In her shock, she leaned back too far in the chair and fell over. Luckily, she landed on a pile of dirty laundry. "How dare you open my door without knocking?" Courtney screamed, throwing a dirty sock at Adam.

"It's not like you would have heard me knocking anyway, with your music so loud."

"That's my business, not yours."

"No, Courtney," Adam said. "It's everyone's business."

Patrick watched with his jaw hanging open.

"While you were listening to your music and typing on your precious cell phone," Adam continued, "your little dog got loose. Do you know where I found her?"

"She got loose?" Courtney asked.

"She was across the street with Arabella Spinelli. She was playing with this stupid purple scarf all afternoon. What if it hadn't been Belle? What if it had been someone mean? Someone like Mister Frostburg?"

Courtney blushed. "He doesn't live here anymore," Courtney said, finally getting up from her pile of laundry.

"That's not the point."

"You know what I heard?" Courtney asked, changing the subject.

"What?"

"I heard that Ms. Paulus read an article about you in front of the whole class. Marnie saw the whole thing. She texted Aileen, who told me all about it. Marnie says you tripped walking up the aisle. What a klutz."

"You'd better stop spreading rumors about me," Adam said, his face red.

"I can't help it if you tripped. I'm just telling what happened."

"I didn't trip. Marnie tripped me," Adam continued.

"Marnie? She would never do anything like that." Courtney laughed. "Hey, Adam?" she asked, changing the subject. "What are you doing for Halloween?"

"I don't know, why?"

"JJ is planning some *really fun stuff*. I mean, we're not going trick-or-treating. That's just for babies. But you're probably trick-or-treating, aren't you?"

Adam didn't say anything, and Courtney turned to Patrick.

"We were planning on it," Patrick said. "I was going to be a goblin. Adam hasn't decided yet, but he'll probably be Logan Zephyr."

Courtney laughed. Adam gave Patrick a look of annoyance.

"Don't give her any information," Adam said. "She'll only use it against us."

Patrick frowned.

"Anyway," Courtney said. "Marnie said you had some girls at school ask you to take them to the Harvest Dance. How cute. What were their names again?" Courtney checked her cell phone for an old text message. "That's right—Olivia. Adam and Olivia sitting in a tree, K-I-S-S-I-N-G..." Courtney laughed again.

Adam crossed his arms. His face grew redder. "I told you to stop being mean to me," he yelled.

Patrick took another step backward.

"Or else what?" Courtney said. She sounded meaner than ever.

"Or else I'll tell Mom and Dad that you let Sapphie get loose."

"Go ahead and tell them," Courtney said. "Everyone knows Sapphie is full of trouble. They wouldn't blame me."

"Then I'll tell them about JJ. I'm sure they'd be interested in knowing that you've been hanging out with a high schooler."

"He's only in tenth grade, though," Courtney said.

"Mom and Dad wouldn't care. They'd take away your cell phone in a heartbeat, and you know it. Then you could kiss all your Halloween plans goodbye."

"Adam, you can't tell them," Courtney said. The meanness had melted from of her voice. She tried to sound as kind and innocent as possible.

"I don't know, Courtney," Adam said. "It's a pretty big secret to be hiding..."

"Please?" Courtney asked. "Please, please, please!"

Adam licked his lips, enjoying having the upper hand. "I'll keep your secret for now, but you've got to stop being mean to me."

"Fine."

"Tell Aileen and Marnie, too," Adam said.

"I can't control what they do," Courtney huffed.

"Well, then maybe I can't control what I tell Mom and Dad about JJ." Adam crossed his arms, daring her to refuse.

Courtney's eyes narrowed into little slits that reminded Adam of snake's eyes, and he shivered just a little.

"Fine," she said grudgingly.

The pair had been so busy fighting they didn't hear Mr. Hollinger walking down the hall with the puppies.

Patrick breathed a loud sigh of relief.

"Hey, kids," Mr. Hollinger said.

Adam and Courtney nearly jumped out of their skins. Zeph jumped on Adam. Sapphie ran up to Courtney, took a flying leap into her arms, and kissed Courtney's face.

"Hello, Patrick," Mr. Hollinger said. "Everything all right up here? I thought I heard yelling."

"Just having a *discussion*," Adam said. "You know how Courtney is."

Courtney opened her mouth to respond, but Adam shot her a dirty look and Courtney stayed quiet.

"Did you work everything out?" Mr. Hollinger asked.

"Yes," Adam and Courtney muttered in unison.

"You sure?" he asked, looking at Patrick.

"Yes."

"Good," Mr. Hollinger said. "Besides, it's rude to argue when we have a guest over." He put a hand on Patrick's shoulder. "Anyway, Mom just called. She's on her way home and picked up a couple of pizzas. We'd better get washed up for dinner, and then you can tell me all about baseball practice.

"Hey," he added, "where did Sapphie get that purple scarf?"

Courtney looked at Adam, but neither answered.

"Arabella gave it to her," Adam said, hoping he wouldn't have to say any more.

Mr. Hollinger nodded. "She's such a nice neighbor, isn't she?"

Adam and Patrick exchanged uneasy glances.

"Anyway," Mr. Hollinger said, "let's get ready for dinner."

The puppies followed Mr. Hollinger downstairs. Patrick followed.

Adam shot Courtney a dirty look before he followed. For the first time in his life, he had real power over Courtney. As long as she wanted to keep JJ a secret from her parents, Adam could get his way. For the first time in his life, Courtney couldn't boss him around.

Adam couldn't have been happier.

~ FOURTEEN ~
A Tough Road Ahead

The next day, Coach Harris kept practice short. The team had a game on Saturday, so he said he'd take it easy on Thursday and Friday—especially for the two pitchers. Coach hit some grounders to the infielders to keep them on their toes and hit a few pop-ups to the outfielders to keep them limber. He had his two pitchers, Greg and Adam, practice in the bull pen. Then he pitched to the boys, letting them each hit a few balls before calling them all together.

He knelt down, chomping on his gum while the boys gathered around. "Reds," he said, looking at each sweaty face. "Who's going to win on Saturday?"

"Us!" The team cheered in unison.

Their next game would be against local rivals, the York White Sox. Even though the White Sox had a weak infield, they were decent batters. Still, when they played the Sox before, they won easily.

"Darn right we're going to win," Coach said. "This is news to no one here, but it'll be news to our friends in York. They just don't know it yet."

The boys exchanged high-fives.

"Now, I'm not saying they're going to hand us a win," Coach Harris continued. "We have to work for everything we get. But if we all play our best, we shouldn't have any problems with this win. The Lancaster Reds are gonna be the Southeastern Regional Champs."

The team cheered.

"How 'bout the team after that?" Austin, who played third base, asked.

"Well," Coach Harris mused, "after we win against the White Sox..." He chomped on his gum some more and studied his clip board. "I predict the next team we'll play are the Scranton Sliders." He paused. "And if we make it to the finals, we'll probably face... the Altoona Angels."

All the boys gasped. They hadn't heard much about the Sliders, but everyone had heard of the Altoona Angels.

"It's not fair that we have to play the Angels," Austin moaned.

"Yeah," agreed Patrick.

Coach Harris frowned at his team. "You'll all be *lucky* to get the chance to play them," he said. "If we make it that far..." He chomped on his gum. "No, *when* we make it that far, it means we'll be one of the top two teams in the state. Sure, the Angels will be tough to beat, but nothing worthwhile is ever easy. Come on, boys, where's that winning spirit?"

The team moped.

Coach Harris frowned again. "The way you're all carrying on, we might lose on Saturday."

"But the Angels..." Tom complained.

"Everyone knows they all have private batting coaches," Patrick mumbled.

"We'll do the best with what we have. That's all anyone can ever do." Coach tried to cheer them up. "You can buy private coaching lessons, but you know what? You can't buy heart. You can't buy passion or love for this game. If—no, *when* we win Saturday's game, we've got two busy weekends coming up. First, we'll have the three-game series, probably against the Sliders. Then we'll have the first game of the final pairing in the series, probably against the Angels. If we tie with one win each during the first two games, we'll have the third game on Saturday afternoon."

"We'll never make it to the third game," Tom said.

"Yeah," Adam agreed. "Playing the Angels we'll be whipped so bad we'll be back in plenty of time for me to go to the Harvest Dance." Adam shook his head. "No. I can't go to that dance," he muttered. Then, he said louder, "We're not going to be defeated. We're going to win."

"That's the spirit," Coach Harris said. "You boys keep an open schedule and an open mind. Who feels like beating some Angels?"

"We do!" Greg, their starting pitcher, cheered. He often took charge of the team, and was able to get the other boys to rally. "Red Rose! Everybody knows!" he shouted, starting the team's cheer.

"We come to the field to defeat our foes!" the rest of the team shouted, finishing the cheer.

Coach Harris clapped, and the boys recited the cheer over and over. By the end of the third repetition, everyone on the team was smiling.

"Who's got spirit? Who's got heart?" Coach asked, jumping to his feet.

"We do!" the team cheered, throwing their red caps high in the air.

~ * ~

After practice, Coach Harris drove Adam and Patrick to Adam's house. Today, Adam promised to rake leaves for Belle, and Patrick wanted to come along.

"I may be late picking you up, Patrick," Coach said. "I hope that's all right? I have a league meeting this evening for coaches of teams in the final games, and it might run late. Adam, tell your parents thank you for watching Patrick while I'm gone."

"No problem," Adam said. "We were planning on raking leaves for a neighbor, anyway."

"That's nice," Coach Harris said. He slapped Adam's arm. "Build up your muscles for the game."

Adam and Patrick exchanged glances. No need to tell him about fortune telling or witches just yet.

Coach Harris smiled at the boys, waved, and drove down the road.

Adam and Patrick stood at the edge of the driveway, staring at Arabella's house on the hill. It loomed above them like a haunted mansion, blocking the setting sun from view. The wind picked up, sending lonely leaves swirling in the air.

"You ready to go over there?" Adam asked.

"Are you nervous?" Patrick asked.

"A little," Adam admitted. "But I just want to get this over with. If she *is* a witch, I guess it's best to find out sooner than later."

"That's true," Patrick said.

"Are you still going to get your fortune read? It was all you could talk about yesterday."

"I don't know," Patrick said nervously. "Maybe I really *should* help you rake leaves instead."

Adam nodded. "Good idea. Let's get Zeph before we head over."

Inside, Courtney was actually in the kitchen, rather than her room. "Hi Adam," she said, looking up from her position on the floor, where she was brushing Sapphie.

Zeph ran up to Adam with his characteristic howl. His coat looked shiny.

"Did you brush Zeph?" Adam asked Courtney.

"Maybe," she said.

"Why?"

"I just thought I'd do something nice for my favorite little brother," she said.

"You mean your *only* brother," Adam corrected. "I think you just don't want Mom or Dad to know you let Sapphie get loose. Or that you're planning on hanging out with JJ on Halloween..."

"Shhh," Courtney whispered. "I thought we had a deal."

"We do," Adam said. "As long as you keep treating me nicely." Adam smiled. He *loved* the fact that Courtney had to do what he said. "In fact," Adam said, "it's my turn to vacuum upstairs, but I'm too busy this week with practice and raking leaves for the neighbors. Do you think you could vacuum for me?"

Courtney's eyebrows drew into a scowl. She opened up her mouth as if she was going to yell, but stopped suddenly. "Of course I can vacuum for you," she said through clenched teeth. "It would be my pleasure." She forced a smile.

"Thanks, Courtney," Adam said, rubbing his victory in her face. "I'm off to rake leaves. Come on, Zeph."

Sapphie gave one glance at Zeph and then turned back to Courtney, basking in all of her Person's attention.

~ * ~

Adam, Patrick, and Zeph walked up the long, hilly driveway to Arabella Spinelli's house. As they reached the top of the hill, the setting sun made long, thin shadows along the drive. In the wind, one of the shutters on the second floor creaked.

"Nice touch," Patrick said.

"I think it's kind of creepy. Like in a scary movie," Adam added.

They stepped onto the front porch. Three pumpkins decorated the doorstep, and a black cat decoration that said *Happy Halloween* hung on the door.

"At least it's not a witch," Patrick said.

Adam shrugged.

Zeph sniffed at the three pumpkins, approaching them as cautiously as possible. Adam and Patrick watched as he investigated. Finally, after sniffing each one, he sat down and let out a very loud howl.

Adam patted the pup's head. "It's okay, Zeph. They're just pumpkins." Zeph cocked his head. "Pumpkins," Adam repeated.

Adam raised a fist to knock on the door, but before his fist touched the door, it opened. Adam nearly jumped out of his skin. There was Cassandra, dressed in her strange black velvet cape, standing at the door with a strange look on her face. Once again, she cleared her throat. Then she closed her eyes and raised her hands.

She's getting ready to chant a spell, Adam thought.

"When shall we three meet again?" she asked. "In thunder, lightning, or in rain?"

Adam looked at Patrick. Both boys took a step back.

Cassandra opened her eyes and giggled. "Scary, huh?" Cassandra said. "Belle told me you'd be here."

Adam whispered to Patrick, "I told you she was weird."

"You're probably here for a fortune telling," Cassandra said. "Come in, come in."

"Actually," said Adam, not wanting to set a foot inside the strange house, "I'm just here to rake leaves."

"Ah," Cassandra said. "There's a rake in the back. But *you*," she said, turning to Patrick. "*You* must be here for a fortune telling."

"I..." Patrick gulped. Before he could answer, Cassandra reached out with one hand and pulled Patrick inside, shutting the door behind her.

Adam and Zeph were left standing on the porch, wondering what would become of their friend.

~ FIFTEEN ~
A Suspicious Purple Notebook

Adam and Zeph wandered into the back yard. There were two rakes leaning against a large tree. Zeph sniffed the rakes and then backed away.

"It's okay, Zeph," Adam said. "They're just rakes. The sooner we finish the better."

He picked up a rake, but Zeph didn't like it one bit. He hurried away, hiding beneath the picnic table on the patio.

Adam shook his head, glad the notorious shed had been removed after Mr. Frostburg's arrest. He sighed and began to rake. It was an easy job, and he didn't understand why Cassandra and Arabella would rather pay him to rake than do it themselves.

"I wonder where they want me to put these leaves when I'm done..." Adam muttered.

"You can put them in that large paper bag over there."

Adam's heart jumped in his chest. Sitting on the patio was Arabella Spinelli. She was dressed in her usual skirt and flowing top. As before, she had on lots of colorful jewelry. This time, her hair was tied in a black bandana with two thick braids flowing down her back.

Had she been there the whole time?

"I didn't mean to scare you."

"Uh, no, uh, you didn't," Adam said, his heart still pounding.

Belle took out a small digital camera. "Do you mind?" she asked. "I just love taking pictures."

"You want a picture of *me*?" Adam asked.

"Sure, why not?"

"I guess it would be okay," Adam said.

She held up the camera with her eye at the viewfinder, but she did not snap a picture. Finally, she answered Adam's quizzical expression.

"Just act natural." She laughed. "I'm trying to get a picture of you doing something natural. Not a picture where you're posing. Just rake leaves. When I see the shot I like, I'll take it. I want to get one of you and Zeph together."

Adam shrugged. He sure wished Patrick were here to witness how weird Belle was being. He continued raking leaves and tried not to look at her, but he couldn't help it. Every once in a while he stole a glance. She just kept sitting there, camera ready to click, watching Adam rake leaves.

Finally, when Adam had raked a sizable pile of leaves, Zeph crept out from under the picnic table and approached the leaf pile. He stayed behind it, making sure to keep away from the rake. After Zeph emerged, Belle started taking pictures. Adam tried not to look up.

When she was done, she took out a purple notebook and scribbled in it quickly. Adam wanted to ask what she was doing, but he didn't. He figured as long as she was distracted with her notebook, she wasn't focusing her attention on him.

When she was done writing, Belle spoke again.

"If you get tired, I have some more hot cider mulling on the stove."

"Thanks," Adam said.

He raked in silence for a while.

"So what are your Halloween plans?" she asked, finally.

"Um..." Adam tried to think. He didn't want to tell her too much. What if she *was* a witch?

"Halloween's my favorite holiday, you know. I love the autumn decorations, the dark color of leaves, the crisp weather, the creepy chill in the air."

Now Adam *really* wished Patrick were here to witness this.

"I guess Halloween's okay," Adam said.

"Are you going trick-or-treating?"

"Probably," Adam said.

"What are you dressing as?"

"Probably Logan Zephyr," he said.

"The space explorer, right?"

Adam's jaw dropped. "How did you know that?"

Belle smiled. "I know things," she said. "I figured that's where Zeph got his name, right? After Logan Zephyr, the famous explorer."

Zeph barked once.

"I guess I'm right, huh Zeph?" Belle said. She opened her purple notebook again and jotted something down. "And is Courtney going trick-or-treating with you?" she asked.

"No," Adam said. "She's too cool for that. That's all I can say."

"That's all you can say?"

"I've already told you all I can," Adam explained.

"What do you mean?"

Adam's ears felt as if they just caught fire. He wasn't supposed to talk about Courtney's Halloween plans. If Courtney found out that he told anyone, she would stop being so nice to him.

"Courtney and I made a deal, and I'm holding to my end of the bargain."

"Is Courtney making secret plans?" Belle asked.

Adam remained quiet, focusing on the leaves.

"You're allowed to answer 'yes' or 'no' questions, aren't you? *That* certainly wouldn't be considered telling on her."

Adam stayed quiet. As long as he didn't tell anyone, Courtney had to be nice to him. This was the first time in years that he and his sister were getting along for extended periods of time. He didn't want to ruin it.

"How about this? If the answer is yes, you just keep raking leaves, and if the answer is no, drop your rake. Okay?"

Adam continued raking.

"Does that mean you agree?" Belle asked.

Adam continued raking.

"Does that mean you're ignoring me?"

Adam took a deep breath and dropped the rake. He didn't want to tattle on his sister, but he sure would feel better if he could just share his secret with *someone*.

"Is Courtney making secret Halloween plans?" Belle asked.

Adam continued to rake.

"Is she hanging out with people your parents don't know about?"

Adam continued raking.

"Is she doing drugs?"

Adam looked right at Arabella, his face blushing at the topic. "I don't think so," he said. He forgot he wasn't supposed to be answering, so he dropped his rake. As stupid as Courtney was, Adam knew she wasn't doing drugs.

Adam picked up his rake.

"Do you know what Courtney's plans are for Halloween?" Belle asked.

Adam started raking again.

"I know it's tough because you promised you'd keep Courtney's secret," Belle said, "but maybe you should tell your parents. She might end up doing something she'll regret later."

Adam kept quiet.

"These people she's hanging out with... are they from her school?"

"Some of them," Adam said.

"Are any of them... older?" Belle asked.

"I can't answer that," Adam said.

"Are any of them in high school?"

Adam looked Belle directly in the eye and then continued raking. Belle jotted down some notes in her purple notebook.

Finally, she said, "I think you've done enough raking for today. You don't want to get tired out for your game. Let's see... today's Thursday. When's your next game?"

"Saturday against York," Adam muttered. His stomach was starting to hurt. Had he already told Belle too much about Courtney?

Belle jotted something down in her notebook. "Why don't you come back on Sunday to rake the rest of the yard?"

Adam nodded.

"While you're raking that pile into the lawn bag, I'll get you some cider. And I'll see if Patrick and Cassie are done with the fortune telling."

Belle disappeared inside just as Patrick emerged. Zeph ran up to greet him. Patrick pet Zeph on the head, but he seemed dazed.

"Patrick, are you okay?" Adam asked.

Patrick stumbled over to Adam. He held open the lawn bag so Adam could rake the leaves into it. While he did so, he whispered to Adam.

"I got my fortune read," he said.

"And?"

"That Cassandra is one weird person."

"I told you she was weird," Adam said. "What did she say?"

"First of all, who in their right mind wears a cape? And all that weird jewelry? Listen, Adam, I really think these two are witches."

"You should've seen how weird Belle was while I raked the leaves. She had a digital camera, but she would only take pictures of me when I wasn't looking."

"Maybe she was putting a spell on you?" Patrick suggested. "I'll bet modern witches use electronics in their spells. Do you feel any different?"

"A little tired, maybe," Adam admitted.

"Maybe that's the start of a spell?"

Both boys glanced at the door to make sure neither Cassandra nor Belle could hear them.

"What did Cassandra tell you about your future?"

"She said that I'll, um, we'll be facing three challenges. One was danger. Something big and white."

"Big and white? Does she mean the White Sox? They shouldn't be any threat to us."

"She said it might not be the White Sox. She said it seemed more dangerous than a baseball team."

"Hmm." Adam continued to rake leaves into the bag, but slowly so they'd have more time to talk.

"She said it would be after the sun sets."

"That's kind of creepy," Adam admitted. "Did she say anything about Saturday's game? Or did she mention the Altoona Angels? Or the Scranton Sliders?"

"She said another of the three challenges seemed like a bird. Something with wings."

"Like the Altoona Angels?" Adam asked.

Patrick shrugged. "My dad said we'd probably be playing them—"

"What was the third challenge she said we'd face?"

Patrick tried to remember. "Oh yeah," he said. "This one was weird. She said it was a masquerade ball."

"A masquerade ball? What does that have to do with Autumn League? Did she tell you whether we'd win at the end of our season?"

"She said we'd be proud at the end of the season."

"Does that mean we'll win?"

Patrick shrugged. "She told me not to read into anything. She said just to play our best, and at the end of the season, we'd be proud of our performance."

"That doesn't tell us much of anything."

"I know," Patrick agreed. "But I'm concerned about this 'big white threat' that Cassandra warned me about."

"It's probably just nonsense."

"Let's hope so."

The wind picked up, causing a whirlwind of leaves to brush up against Adam and Patrick. Zeph growled and nipped at the leaves.

"Oh, I forgot to tell you," Adam said. "Belle's got this purple notebook that she..."

But Adam couldn't finish telling Patrick about the notebook because Belle and Cassandra came out to the patio with four mugs of mulled apple cider. The whirlwind of leaves dropped to the ground immediately.

"Drink fast," Adam and Patrick whispered in unison.

"You don't think it's a potion, do you?" Patrick asked.

"There's no way to tell," Adam said. "But it wasn't last time."

They walked slowly to the patio. Zeph hung back behind Adam.

"What's wrong with Zeph?" Belle asked. "He's been so mellow."

"I'm just feeling tired," Adam said. "And Zeph can usually tell when I need sleep. Besides, he's afraid of rakes. And pumpkins. And about a dozen other things."

"Like what?" she asked.

"Like witches," Patrick said a bit too loudly.

"I see." She pulled out her purple notebook and jotted something down with her purple pen, covered in rhinestones—just like Courtney's cell phone.

"Do you boys believe in witches?" she asked

"Yes," Patrick said at the same time that Adam answered, "No."

"I'm sure Zeph doesn't have to worry about witches. There aren't any witches around here, right, Cassie?"

Cassandra started laughing, and Belle joined in. Before long, the two of them were cackling.

The boys exchanged knowing glances.

"So what do you boys like to do for fun?" Belle asked after she stopped laughing. She spoke as if she were interviewing them. "I mean, when you aren't at school, or raking leaves, or playing baseball?"

"Comics," the boys answered in unison.

"We love going to Carlton's Comics," Patrick said.

Adam poked him in the ribs. Patrick had a habit of giving away too much information, especially to Arabella Spinelli.

"Carlton's Comics," Belle repeated as she wrote something down.

"That's the place downtown, isn't it?" Cassandra asked.

"Yes," Patrick said.

"I work just down the street from there," Cassandra said. Belle and Cassandra made eye contact and grinned strangely.

"Well," Adam said, gulping the rest of his cider even though it burned his tongue, "I'd better head home. Thanks for the cider. I'll finish raking on Sunday."

Belle seemed surprised at his abrupt exit, but Adam didn't care.

"Want me to carry the bag of leaves down to the end of your driveway?" he asked.

"No," Belle said. "We'll take care of the leaves."

"Okay," Adam said. "Come on, Zeph. Come on, Patrick."

Surprised, Patrick gulped down the rest of his cider and joined Adam in a fast walk back to the Hollinger's home. Adam turned back only once, just long enough to see Cassandra and Belle watching him as carefully as hawks tracking their prey.

~ SIXTEEN ~
Bad News in the Back Yard

On his front porch, Adam stopped with his hand on the doorknob. "Patrick," he said quietly, "we've got to find a copy of *Logan Zephyr and the Space Sorceress*."

"Why?" Patrick asked.

"We should compare notes. See if Belle and Cassandra have anything in common with the sorceress Logan Zephyr had to face."

"That's true," Patrick said.

"I've had good luck in the past relying on my *Riley Couth* comics for pointers on detective work. Maybe *Logan Zephyr* can help us this time."

Patrick nodded.

Adam opened the door quietly and stuck his head inside. "It sounds like dinner's not ready yet," Adam told Patrick. "Let's take Zeph to the back yard."

"Why?" Patrick asked.

Adam closed the door quietly, holding it so it wouldn't slam. "I want to talk about Belle and Cassandra. My parents really like them, and I don't want to talk about them being *you-know-what's* in front of my parents. Besides, Courtney's usually up in her room, so if we're in the back yard, she won't be able to bother us."

"Suits me," Patrick said, following Adam to the back yard.

"What else happened while Cassandra was reading your fortune?" Adam asked.

The two boys opened the gate to the back yard. Patrick didn't have time to answer because when Adam opened the gate, Sapphie flew out.

Patrick tried to catch her, but Sapphie was too fast, and too low to the ground.

"Sapphie, come back," Adam called.

Sapphie ran wide circles around Patrick, but she wouldn't stop, and she wouldn't listen.

"Courtney's the only one who can ever control her," Adam said. "And even then, Sapphie barely listens."

"Sapphie," Courtney yelled from the back yard.

Sapphie's ears pricked up, and she stopped running in circles. With a single, shrill yelp, Sapphie returned to the back yard and took a running leap into Courtney's arms.

Adam and Patrick joined Courtney in the back and quickly closed the gate. But they were surprised by what they saw.

There, sitting in the back corner of the yard, were some of Courtney's friends. Patrick and Adam recognized Aileen and Meghan from school, but there was a boy there that neither recognized.

"Probably JJ," Adam whispered to Patrick.

"What are you two doing here?" Courtney asked, and Adam immediately recognized her mean tone of voice.

"Um, I *live* here," Adam said, gearing up for an argument.

Patrick shook his head and shuffled over to the tire swing on the other side of the yard.

Sapphie jumped down and barked at Zeph. Wagging her tail, she dashed behind the compost pile. Zeph followed, sneaking away while Courtney and Adam were fighting.

~ * ~

"Zeph," Sapphie squealed.

"Shhh," Zeph warned, pointing his nose at all the people in the yard.

"Oh, Zeph. They can't hear us behind this compost pile. Besides, they're too busy fighting. Before you got here, I was working on widening my escape hole, and no one even noticed."

Zeph craned his neck around the compost pile. Sapphie was right. Adam and Courtney were busy fighting. Aileen and Meghan were busy looking at their cell phones, and JJ watched Adam with a smirk.

Zeph couldn't help but growl.

"I don't like him either," Sapphie said. "I wish JJ would just go away."

"You don't like him?" Zeph asked. "I'm surprised. You like *everyone*."

"How could I like him? Whenever he's around, all of Courtney's attention is on him, and *none* of her attention is on me, me, *me*!"

"Hmm," Zeph thought.

"That's why I started widening my escape hole in the first place. I was just trying to get Courtney's attention. But she didn't even notice." Sapphie plopped down on the ground. Zeph had never seen her so sad.

"I don't like JJ either," Zeph said.

"Why?" Sapphie asked. "Is it because he takes Adam's attention away from you?"

"No," Zeph said. "In fact, Adam doesn't seem to like him very much."

The puppies peeked around the corner of the compost pile. Adam and Courtney were having a heated discussion, and every time Courtney made a point, JJ laughed at Adam.

"Then why don't you like JJ?" Sapphie asked.

"I don't know," Zeph said. "There are too many new people. JJ, Arabella, Cassandra. They all seem so strange. It's confusing."

Sapphie wagged her tail and bit down on Zeph's ear.

"Ouch," Zeph cried. "What was that for?"

"That was for your attitude about Arabella and Cassandra. They're so nice. How could you think they're not? No one else in the *world* ever gave me a purple scarf."

"Just because someone gives you a purple scarf doesn't mean they're nice."

"Sure it does, Zeph," Sapphie said. She tugged on his ear once more before charging into the yard to try and earn Courtney's attention.

But Courtney was too busy fighting with Adam to notice her messy little puppy.

"Stay out of *my* back yard," Courtney said.

"It's my back yard, too, Courtney," Adam said. "What are *you* doing here? You're usually locked up in your room."

"I couldn't very well sneak JJ up into my room, now, could I?" Courtney was all attitude.

"You could get in so much trouble if Mom and Dad find out that JJ's even here."

"I know, stupid," Courtney said. "Which is why you aren't going to tell them."

"Well, maybe I should, especially since you keep calling me *stupid*."

"Let's see what JJ has to say about it."

From the corner of the yard, JJ approached. He looked much older than Courtney. He wore a distressed blue jean jacket, its collar pulled up. His dark hair was long and spiky, and he even had some fuzzy stubble on his chin, as if he were trying to grow a beard.

"Did I hear my name?" he asked. His voice was deep, and the way he spoke was intimidating.

"No," Adam said.

"Yes," Courtney said. "JJ, Adam was just about to tell my parents that you're here."

"Hmm," JJ mused. "That doesn't sound like a good idea. Nope, not at all."

Patrick hopped off the tire swing and approached Adam, but he did so hesitantly.

"Courtney, you promised to stop being so mean to me," Adam said. "I'm tired of you always tormenting me."

"Sounds like a baby to me," JJ said. "Aileen, why don't you come over here and look at the baby?"

To Adam's horror, Aileen approached, followed by Meghan.

Aileen laughed. "Maybe I'll have an embarrassing story about you to tell my sister. Marnie would love to hear how you got your butt kicked by a tenth grader."

Adam and Patrick froze.

"Show them what they taught you in gym class," Courtney said.

"What gym class?" Adam asked.

"High school gym classes are so much better than baby gym classes," JJ said. "I'm taking kick boxing." JJ took a few steps back, then approached the compost pile. "Imagine that half-rotted watermelon is your head," he said arrogantly and gave a swift, high kick to the compost pile. The watermelon split into pieces and fell to the ground. JJ laughed. "That's what I think of you."

Sapphie licked the watermelon rind that had fallen at her feet. Zeph came running from behind the compost pile. He jumped between Adam and JJ. The fur on his neck raised high in the air, and he let out a long, rolling growl. Sapphie abandoned the watermelon and followed suit.

"Maybe we should go inside," Patrick said.

But Adam was mad.

"No, Patrick." He turned to Courtney. "I'm tired of this. This is my house, too. You can't always boss me around."

"Yes, I can," Courtney said.

"Can't," Adam said.

"Can," Courtney shouted.

They went back and forth for a minute longer. The dogs joined in, barking loudly each time one of them spoke. Patrick, JJ, and the girls exchanged bored glances. Finally, a car pulled in the driveway.

"That's Courtney's dad," Aileen shouted to JJ. "You'd better get out of here."

JJ wasted no time. He took a running leap, cleared the fence, and disappeared into the tree line.

Courtney stopped yelling at Adam long enough to watch. "Isn't he so cool?" she asked.

Adam huffed.

Mr. Hollinger got out of the car and approached the fence.

"What are you all up to?" he asked. "It looks like a party back here."

"No party," Courtney said a little too loudly and a little too quickly.

"No party, eh?" Mr. Hollinger seemed suspicious. He turned to Adam. "Adam, I know I can trust you. You guys weren't doing anything you weren't supposed to be, were you?"

Adam swallowed hard.

"Well?" Mr. Hollinger asked.

Behind Mr. Hollinger's back, Aileen made a sour face at Adam. She ran one finger along her throat in a threatening gesture. Adam knew she and Courtney would be mad if he told.

"We weren't doing anything bad," Adam said. "Just hanging out with the dogs."

"Patrick?" Mr. Hollinger asked. His brow rose in suspicion.

Patrick nodded in agreement.

Zeph barked frantically. Sapphie ran to the fence, pawing at the spot JJ had jumped over.

"All this excitement sure is getting to the dogs," Mr. Hollinger said. "Let's get them inside and see if dinner's ready. Courtney, are your friends staying, too?"

"No," Courtney said. "They were just leaving."

Adam went out the gate and followed his dad to the front yard before there were any more dirty looks from Courtney or her friends. As he approached the front door, he saw a sight that made him shudder.

There, standing on her hilly driveway, was Arabella Spinelli. Her arms were crossed, and she stared intently across the street at the Hollinger's fence, right at the place where JJ had jumped.

~ SEVENTEEN ~
Butterflies with the Sunrise

On Saturday, Adam woke with butterflies in his stomach. In a few hours the Lancaster Reds would play the York White Sox. Just four teams remained in the playoffs. Although the Reds had beaten the White Sox before, Adam had a strange feeling about today's game.

He awoke before everyone else and let Zeph and Sapphie out in the back yard. Sapphie kept stretching and yawning. It was clear she wanted to go back to sleep. Zeph, on the other hand, seemed excited and happy to be awake so early.

"Let's get you inside." Adam grabbed a towel to wipe the dew off Sapphie's paws.

As tired as Sapphie was, just the sight of the towel made her wild. She charged at Adam, snapping at the towel as she passed. Adam felt like a bull-fighter, flapping the towel and jumping out of Sapphie's way as if she were a charging bull.

Each time Adam bent down to scoop Sapphie up, she turned the other way. Sapphie was so low to the ground that it was difficult for Adam to grab her. Before long, Sapphie's energy rubbed off on Zeph, and both dogs circled the yard wildly, chasing each other and barking wildly.

Their barking must have awoken the whole house because when Adam looked up, his father appeared on the patio with a mug of coffee. He looked tired, and his hair stuck straight up, as if he had just gotten out of bed.

"Hey, sport," he mumbled to Adam. "You're up early."

"Yeah," Adam said. "I couldn't sleep. Sorry if the dogs woke you."

"Actually, it wasn't the dogs," Mr. Hollinger said. "It was the phone. Coach Harris called. Greg came down with something. He's been sick to his stomach since early this morning, and won't be able to pitch today. Coach wants to know how you feel about pitching the whole game."

"What did Greg come down with?" Adam asked. "Maybe it'll pass and he can pitch the last few innings." The butterflies lurched in Adam's stomach.

"From what Coach said," Mr. Hollinger explained, "it sounds like an early case of the flu. Or maybe food poisoning. Sounds like Greg won't be getting out of bed anytime today."

"What about Bryce? Maybe his arm's good enough to pitch."

Mr. Hollinger shook his head. "Bryce is out for the season. A break takes a while to heal. Besides, he hasn't been training, and his doctor told him no more baseball until next season."

"Hmm," Adam wondered. He loved pitching, but as the only pitcher of the game, the whole team would be depending on him. And that meant a *lot* of pitching.

"You feeling up to it?" Mr. Hollinger asked.

"What if I don't want to?" Adam asked.

Mr. Hollinger frowned. "Coach told me he knows it's a lot of pressure for you. And it's a lot of work. He asked my permission to let you pitch the whole time, and I said I would leave it up to you."

"And if I say no?" Adam felt beads of sweat forming on his brow.

"Coach says the alternative is for the Reds to forfeit."

"And lose to the White Sox? The team would hate me for it. That means York would become Southeast Champions, and not Lancaster!" Adam's mind raced.

Cassandra had told Patrick to beware of something big and white. Maybe she meant the White Sox. Maybe Adam was going to lose the game for his team. Adam grabbed his gut.

Mr. Hollinger took a sip of coffee. *How can he drink at a time like this?*

"I told Coach you'd give him a call in a few minutes."

"I don't know if I can do it," Adam said. "If we're going to lose, it'd be easier just to forfeit the game."

Mr. Hollinger pulled together two lawn chairs and sat down on the patio. He was wearing pajamas, and his slippers were on the wrong feet. But Adam was too nervous to laugh.

"Adam," Mr. Hollinger said once Adam took a seat. "You're a great pitcher. There's a reason Coach Harris chose you as alternate. He saw something in you. I know it's tiring, but if anyone can pitch the whole game, it's you. I know you can."

"I *don't* know, Dad."

By this time, Zeph was tired of running in circles, so he jumped onto the patio and plopped down under Adam's chair. Sapphie kept running, widening her circle to run right by Zeph each time she passed the patio.

"Sapphie," Mr. Hollinger said. "Calm down."

But his words seemed to send Sapphie into a frantic frenzy. She continued running in circles around the yard, only this time she ran onto the patio, jumped onto Mr. Hollinger's lap, spilled his coffee, licked his face, jumped down again, and resumed running.

"She's out of control," Adam said. "Courtney's the only one who can calm her."

Mr. Hollinger shook his head. "I'll get Courtney. You stay out here and think about the game. But I'll tell you what I think."

"What's that?" Adam asked.

"You may pitch a flawless game, or you might make some mistakes. But if you don't even try, then you're guaranteed to fail."

"If I pitch and mess up, though, the whole team's going to blame me. And what if I get too tired?"

"It's called a team for a reason," Mr. Hollinger reminded him. "It doesn't depend on just one person. It depends on every person. And you're part of that team. No one's going to blame you if the Reds don't win. The team's asking a lot of you. Everyone knows that."

Adam frowned and nodded. While his dad went inside to get Courtney, Adam bent down to pet Zeph. Sapphie continued barking wildly at Adam and trying to tug on Zeph's ear. Adam tried to ignore the wild puppy while he thought about pitching. No matter what his father said, they were down to the last eight teams. If Adam pitched well, he would be a team star. But if he messed up, the whole team would blame him. And if he refused, the team would forfeit, and then they'd end up blaming him for being a chicken.

While Adam was lost in thought, Courtney came outside, wearing furry pink slippers and purple pajamas.

"Sapphie, come here," she yawned, stooping over.

Sapphie immediately stopped running in circles. Her ears flew back, and she took a running leap into Courtney's arms. Courtney turned to go back inside when she changed her mind. She turned and sat in a lawn chair next to Adam, petting Sapphie on her lap.

"Hey," she said.

"Hey."

"Thanks for not telling on me yesterday."

"Not like I had a choice," Adam said.

Courtney shrugged. "You can't mess with JJ. He's too cool."

"Whatever," Adam said. He was tired of being bossed around by his sister.

"Listen," Courtney said. "Dad told me about your baseball game today. I know you're scared, and I know I give you a hard time... but you're not *always* as dorky as I say you are."

Adam raised one brow.

"I mean, I know I give you a hard time, but you're a pretty good brother."

Adam could hardly believe Courtney was being nice to him.

"I'm just saying..." Courtney sounded nervous—as if she wasn't used to giving compliments. "I'm just saying," she repeated, "that it's pretty cool having a brother in the Autumn League. And if you made it this far as a pitcher, I'm sure you'll do a great job at the game."

Adam smiled. "Thanks, Courtney."

Courtney smiled back, got up, and carried Sapphie inside.

For a moment, Adam wondered why Courtney was being so nice. Was it just that she didn't want Adam telling his parents about JJ? He shook his head and decided it didn't matter. If Courtney wanted to be nice to him for a change, he wasn't going to stop her.

"Well, Zeph," Adam said. "It looks like I'm pitching the whole game today."

Zeph let out a friendly bark and followed Adam inside. At the breakfast table, Mrs. Hollinger had already set out orange juice and toast. Adam could smell scrambled eggs.

"Mmm," he said, and washed his hands.

Mrs. Hollinger smiled. "Adam, I hear that Coach Harris has asked you to pitch the whole game today."

"Yeah," Adam said.

"Have you decided what to tell him?"

"I'm going to do it," Adam said.

"Great. Did you hear that, dear?" Mrs. Hollinger asked her husband, who was in the dining room trying to read through the newspaper before breakfast.

"That's great," Mr. Hollinger said, putting down a newspaper. "We'll all come to watch. Me and Mom..."

"Mom and *I*," Mrs. Hollinger quietly corrected.

"Mom and I will come to watch," Mr. Hollinger said, "and Courtney, and we'll even bring the dogs."

At the breakfast table, Courtney groaned. "Do I have to?" she sighed.

"Yes," Mr. Hollinger called from the dining room.

"But I was gonna hang out with my friends to-day," she complained.

"You were *going to*," Mrs. Hollinger correct-ed. "Not *gonna*."

"Fine," Courtney said. "I am *going to* hang out with my friends today. Is that better?"

"Almost," Mrs. Hollinger said. "You *were* go-ing to hang out with your friends today. But now you are going to come with us to watch Adam pitch."

Courtney's jaw dropped. She took one look at Adam and opened her mouth to complain, but Adam shook his head and raised one brow, letting her know that he knew about JJ. Courtney looked miserable, but picked up her cell phone and started sending text messages.

"You can hang out with them later," Mrs. Hol-linger said. "Adam's game is at eleven. We'll be home later this afternoon."

"Whatever," Courtney said. "At least I'll have my cell phone."

"You know, it might be a nice idea to invite Arabella and Cassandra. I mean, I'm sure they have better things to do on their Saturdays, but it seems neighborly to invite them anyway. It would be fun if they could come along," Mrs. Hollinger said.

Adam's eyes opened in horror. "I don't think we should bother them on the weekend," he said a little too quickly. "Besides, it's kind of early."

"Adam's just saying that because he has a crush on Belle," Courtney announced.

"I do not," Adam shouted back.

He already felt his ears turning red. Having a crush on Belle was the furthest thing from the truth. Why was Courtney always making up lies about him, especially after he had kept her secret?

"So, if you don't have a crush on her, why don't you want her coming?" Courtney asked.

"Because she's a..." Adam knew he couldn't answer. He didn't want his parents, or Courtney, for that matter, knowing he thought Belle was a witch.

"Why?" Courtney added.

"No reason," Adam said.

"Great, then," Mrs. Hollinger said cheerfully. "Courtney, Belle told me the two of you have been texting. Why don't you text her and see if she's awake? And if she is, I'll give her a call."

Adam rolled his eyes and tried to concentrate on not getting nervous for his game.

"Belle's awake," Courtney groaned. "She says you can call her now."

Mrs. Hollinger picked up the portable phone. "These eggs are just about ready," Mrs. Hollinger said. She stirred them with one hand while she dialed the phone with the other. "Good morning, Belle. How are you?" She paused.

"Great. Great. We just wanted to invite you to Adam's baseball game today. It turns out the starting pitcher has the flu, so it looks like Adam will be pitching the whole game. We thought he could use all the fans he could get.

"Of course he'd like you to come along. Oh, and Cassandra too, if she likes. Oh, she's working? That's too bad. Well, you certainly are welcome, dear. Yes, he'll be there, too. Great."

Adam sat frozen in his chair at the kitchen table while he listened to his mother give Arabella directions to the baseball field. He couldn't believe that Arabella was actually coming. Didn't she have better things to do on a Saturday? He'd have to call Patrick for sure.

"Great news, Adam," Mrs. Hollinger said. She had hung up the phone and was carrying a steaming plate of scrambled eggs to the table. "Honey, break-fast's ready," she called into the dining room.

"Let me guess," Adam said. "Arabella's com-ing to the game."

"Yes. Unfortunately, Cassandra can't come. She's working today, but Belle will be there. She said she'll be excited to cheer for you. And she was even more excited when she heard that Zeph was coming along."

At the mention of his name, Zeph barked. Sapphie barked back and jumped onto Courtney's lap.

"Courtney," Mrs. Hollinger scolded. "No pup-pies at the table."

"Fine," Courtney pouted. "I still can't believe you're making me go to Adam's stupid game."

"Courtney," Mrs. Hollinger said. "Let's try to have a positive attitude for once. What did you have to do today that was so important you'd be willing to miss your brother pitch during the state playoffs?"

"Oh, just hanging out," Courtney said.

"I've got an idea," Mrs. Hollinger said. "Why don't you bring your friends to the game? The more fans Adam has, the better. And your friends would have a good time."

As nervous as Adam was, he couldn't help but laugh. He could just imagine JJ showing up at the baseball game. He could picture his parents' reac-tion to his leather boots and spiked hair, and his spiked collar and pierced ear.

"Something funny, Adam?" Courtney asked meanly.

"No," Adam said. "I was thinking of something from my comic book."

Courtney gave him the evil eye. "My friends wouldn't like going to a boring baseball game," Courtney mumbled.

"That's too bad," Mrs. Hollinger said.

Mr. Hollinger finally came in from the dining room. "I finished my paper," he announced, and dropped it into the kitchen recycling bin. He looked at his family as if he had just climbed Mount Everest.

"Hallelujah to that," Mrs. Hollinger joked. "Now sit down and dig in."

"Okay," Mr. Hollinger said. "But Adam first. He's going to need all the energy he can get."

Adam scooped a big helping of eggs onto his plate. He ate quickly, eager to call Coach Harris so he could talk to Patrick.

~ EIGHTEEN ~
Magic at the Game

After breakfast, the Hollingers packed themselves—and the puppies—into the minivan.

"Why do we have to leave so early?" Courtney complained. She shuffled into the back seat.

Her hair was pulled back in a ponytail, and she wore jeans and a t-shirt. Normally, Courtney spent forever getting ready to go out. This morning, there was no time. "It's barely nine o'clock," she whined. "J—I mean, Aileen's still in bed. She must be. She's not answering her text messages."

"Honey," Mrs. Hollinger said. "Adam needs to get there early to warm up. It takes a while to get to the college. It's all the way in York. We might as well all arrive early to get good seats."

"As long as Dad's driving," Courtney added, laughing.

Mr. Hollinger agreed. "The last time you tried to navigate somewhere, we ended up with two puppies."

Even Mrs. Hollinger laughed.

Adam was the last to get into the car. He was carrying his long duffle bag, which contained his bat and glove.

"You look very nice," Mrs. Hollinger told him. "When we get to the college, I want to take lots of pictures."

Adam looked down at his uniform. The Lancaster Reds wore a white shirt with red pinstripes, white pants, and red stirrups. Decorating the jersey was a baseball with a red rose inside of it.

"Thanks," Adam said, smiling.

"Doesn't he look nice, Courtney?" Mrs. Hollinger asked while Adam climbed into the minivan.

Courtney glared at her brother. Adam stared back with defiance and whispered one word to Courtney.

"JJ."

"Yes," Courtney agreed, loudly enough for her mother to hear. "Adam looks very nice today."

~ * ~

When they arrived at the field, Patrick was already waiting. Members of the other team, the York White Sox, were starting to trickle in. Their uniforms were black and white. The "O" in "York" was a white rose.

"Ah," Coach Harris said, inhaling a deep breath of fresh morning air. "It'll be an appropriate game. The Red Rose versus the White Rose. Just like days of old."

"Huh?" Adam asked Patrick.

"Oh," Patrick said, rolling his eyes. "My dad's just a history buff. He was telling me all about it in the car on the way over. Over in England, there were two groups of people that were sort of rivals. They were called the House of Lancaster, which was represented by a red rose, and the House of York, which was represented by the white rose. Dad's all excited that both of our teams are named after a piece of history."

"Oh," Adam said. Though history was one of his favorite subjects in school, this was no time for a lesson.

"Here, check out this dugout," Patrick said. He led Adam down into a real dugout that was partly underground—not like the splintery benches the team normally used at their practice field.

Adam gasped. "It's like a real, professional team's." Both boys jumped into the dugout. Adam stowed his duffle bag underneath the bench. "This is so cool," he said.

Mr. Hollinger came over with a camera. "Smile, boys," he said.

Even though Adam didn't want any distractions before the game, he was glad his dad remembered the camera. He had never been in a real dugout before, and this was something he wanted to remember.

"Look at all those seats," Adam said.

"This is a college field," Mr. Hollinger said. "It's meant to hold a lot of spectators."

Adam nodded nervously.

"Ready to strike 'em out?" Mr. Hollinger asked.

"I guess so," Adam said.

"I *know* so." Mr. Hollinger reached into the dugout to give Adam a fist-bump.

"Da-ad," Adam protested. Mr. Hollinger's new thing was to give fist-bumps instead of handshakes. He thought he was being cool, but it just embarrassed Adam. "Parents don't do that." Adam shook his head.

"Okay, okay," Mr. Hollinger said, and settled for a plain old handshake. "Good luck, sport."

"Thanks, Dad," Adam said. "Good luck with Courtney."

"Oh, she'll be fine," Mr. Hollinger said. "She just told me that some of her friends are going coming to watch."

"What friends?" Adam asked.

"I'm not sure," Mr. Hollinger said. "Why?"

"I just thought..." Adam was afraid of what Courtney and JJ would do if Adam told his dad about them. "Nothing," Adam said finally.

"You sure everything's okay between you and Courtney?" Mr. Hollinger asked.

"Yes," Adam said. "But please don't let Courtney watch Zeph. I don't want him running off."

"Your mom and I will watch him," Mr. Hollinger promised before he walked toward the bleachers.

On the infield, Coach Harris clapped his hands. "Warm up in two minutes," he shouted.

All the boys from the team scrambled into the dugout and grabbed their gloves.

"Ready to pitch?" Patrick slapped Adam on the shoulder.

"Yes," Adam said, "but..."

"But what?"

"We have bigger problems," he said.

"What could possibly be more important than this game?" Patrick asked.

Adam shuddered. "I told you on the phone. My parents invited Belle to watch."

Patrick frowned. "You can't be distracted with that. Maybe she won't come."

"No," Adam said. "She's coming all right. This is the college where she takes classes, anyway. Mom said she's all excited to watch the game."

"Just try to concentrate on pitching."

"But what if she really is a w—"

"We'll figure that out later," Patrick promised. "For now, let's focus on beating these Sox."

Coach Harris came over. "Ready to pitch, Adam?"

Adam nodded.

"Alex," Coach Harris yelled. "Suit up and start warming up with Adam."

Alex, the catcher, nodded.

"Listen," Coach Harris told Adam, "you've got this. You have it in you. You just need to concentrate."

"I hope so." Adam knew he didn't sound too sure of himself.

Coach Harris jumped into the dugout. "Go warm up, Patrick," he said. Patrick nodded and ran to the field. Coach Harris turned to Adam and lowered his voice. "There's something I never told you, Adam. The day I had to choose a starting pitcher, after Bryce broke his arm, I almost chose you."

"Really?" Adam asked.

"Yes. You and Greg were so close, I couldn't decide who to pick. I ended up choosing Greg."

"Why?" Adam asked.

"Since you and Patrick are best friends, I thought it might look bad if I chose you. I thought people might think I was picking favorites. But I think you're just as good as Greg."

Adam smiled. "Really?"

Coach Hollinger patted him on the back. "That's why I put you in every game. Got it?"

Adam nodded. "Got it."

He ran over to join Alex in one of the bullpens. He tried not to look over in the stands, where Zeph, Sapphie, and his family were getting situated. This round of the playoffs was only one game—the four winning teams would progress to the next level. Adam wouldn't have a second chance. He had to block out all distractions.

"You ready for this?" Alex asked Adam. He was all suited up in his catcher gear.

"I am," Adam said.

"All right, then," Coach Harris cheered, chomping on his gum. "Let's go get ready to strike out some Sox."

Adam nodded.

Alex pulled down his mask and took his spot. Adam concentrated hard as he tried every type of pitch. He tried ordinary pitches. He tried pitches so low that the batter would mistake them for balls. He tried splitters, sinkers, breakers, and curve balls. He remembered everything his dad taught him. Each one was nearly perfect.

"Looking good, Adam," Alex said. "Maybe you should give your arm a rest for a while. You'll be pitching all game."

Adam nodded. The rest of the team had been warming up on the field, and they were now headed back to the dugout. Adam and Alex ran back to join them.

"Hollinger," Coach Harris called when the team was seated.

"Yes, Coach?"

"I was watching you warm up. Great job. I've never seen such concentration. Keep it up during the game, and we'll win this for sure."

Adam smiled. *Concentrate*, he told himself.

Coach Harris called the batting order and starting positions. "Now boys," he said. "We've won against the York White Sox once before. It was an easy win, but they look hungry for a win today, so don't expect a cake walk. Nothing in life is handed to you. Today, we can earn our win. Now as you know, Greg is out with the flu, so Adam's pitching the whole game. Boys, I need you to be on your toes out there on the field. Get as many outs as you can.

We don't want to tire out Adam's arm. Now let's win this," he screamed, clapping.

"Whoo!" Patrick yelled.

"Whoo!" the rest of the team shouted.

"Red Rose," Patrick shouted.

"Everybody knows," Adam yelled.

"We come to this field to defeat our foes!" the rest of the team shouted in unison.

"That's the spirit," Coach Harris said, clapping.

On the field, an umpire called for the coaches. "Five minutes," he said.

"Looks like we'll be starting soon," Coach said. "We have more wins than York, so we take the field first. You boys get ready to line up for the Star Spangled Banner." He left to let the umpire inspect the game roster and batting order.

At the umpire's call, the teams lined up on the first and third baselines while one of the students from the community college walked out onto the field. She held a microphone, and everyone in the stands clapped and cheered. She smiled and waved to the crowd. Her hair was tied back in white and red ribbons in honor of the two teams playing. She put the microphone up to her mouth, and everyone quieted while she sang the National Anthem.

Adam watched the sky as she sang. It was a perfect blue, with just a few clouds here and there. The air was cool but not cold—perfect playing weather. Maybe the bad feeling he had that morning was just nerves. As the sun shone on his face and the music swelled in the background, he remembered what Coach Harris told him about his pitching, and he smiled with confidence.

The crowd broke out in applause after the song had finished, and the Reds ran out to the pitcher's mound. They each put a gloved hand into the center of the mound. All at once, they shouted: "Lancaster, Lancaster, Lancaster Reds! Strike 'em and catch 'em and put 'em to bed!" The boys cheered and threw their gloved hands in the air.

Then Coach Harris clapped his hands, and they took their positions, warming up for a moment. Adam threw a few pitches. He took it slow, not wanting to strain a muscle before the game.

"Balls in," the umpire called.

Adam's gut tightened with nerves as he threw the practice ball to the catcher.

"Let's have a batter," the umpire called.

Adam looked at York's dugout. All the boys on the team were standing, their faces peering from inside the dugout. All eyes were on him. Behind the dugout, three boys were warming up with bats while the first batter walked to plate. The batters warming up swung furiously at the air with two bats. They looked like strong hitters.

It seemed to take forever for the batter to make it to home plate. He was a tall boy, probably the tallest on the team, and he tapped the plate with his bat. He looked at Adam with a snarl.

"Let's go Adam," Mr. Hollinger called from the stand.

Adam heard Zeph and Sapphie bark in response. He tried to block them out and focus only on pitching. He decided to start simple with a fastball.

He took a deep breath, focused on his target, and wound up. As he let go of the ball, time seemed to move in slow motion. But as soon as the ball got to home plate, time seemed to move in fast forward. Before Adam could figure out what was happening, he heard the crack of a bat, and the ball was heading straight for him, a hard line drive.

Adam couldn't do anything but duck. He hadn't expected the batter to score a hit from his first pitch. Luckily, Patrick hustled behind Adam and made the catch.

The crowd cheered.

Adam felt out of breath. His hand shook. He'd almost been slammed in the head with a ball. He had been concentrating so hard on pitching that he forgot to pay attention after the ball had been hit.

"You okay, Adam?" Patrick asked, handing him the ball.

"Yeah," Adam said with a shaky voice. "Nice catch.

Patrick slapped him on the shoulder and returned to his position.

"One out," the umpire yelled.

Adam looked up at the electronic scoreboard. It was the first time he'd ever played with one.

"Concentrate, Hollinger," Coach Harris screamed from the sideline.

Adam nodded.

The next batter was much shorter and didn't look as confident. Adam struck him out with a fastball, a slider, and a ball which looked so close to a strike that the batter swung and missed.

"Nice job, Hollinger," Coach Harris called.

The third batter looked strong. He stood at the plate and glared at Adam as if he would knock the cover off the ball. Adam tried to concentrate, but even over the cheering crowd, he heard a dog bark. He knew it was Sapphie. He knew he shouldn't look over, and he told himself just to concentrate on pitching, but he couldn't help it. He stole just one glance at the bleachers, and what he saw made his heart sink.

There was Sapphie, barking at a woman in a flowing red skirt, black shirt, and red scarf tied about her head. Unmistakably, it was Arabella Spinelli. She had come to watch the game.

"Belle," Adam whispered.

She turned to see that Adam was looking at her, and she smiled and waved.

Adam turned back to the batter. He took a deep breath and threw, but it was as if his muscles had lost power. What was meant to be a fastball was probably the slowest pitch he'd thrown all season.

The batter smiled as the ball approached the plate, and he swung with all his might. Adam heard the crack of the bat, and he saw the ball pop up and fly over all the infielders. It was headed beyond the fence, Adam could tell. It was a homerun. Adam watched the ball fly through the air.

But just as Adam started scolding himself for throwing such a slow pitch, he heard his teammates chanting, "George! George! George!"

He turned to see George, one of the outfielders, running with all his might to the fence. As if in slow motion, George knelt down, then sprang up high into the air. Adam—and everyone else in the stands—watched with amazement as George's glove scooped the ball out of the air. He landed hard on his ankle, and then he hit the ground. Everyone paused to see if he was all right.

"Oh no," Coach Harris called. "His ankle!" He ran onto the field. But after a moment, George sat up. With his right hand, he reached into his glove and lifted the ball high above his head for all to see. Then, slowly, he got to his feet. He was okay.

The crowd went wild.

"All right," shouted Coach Harris. "Nice catch, George. Great work, team. Three up, three down. That's just the way we like to do things. Nice work, Hollinger. Good work, everyone."

The team ran to the dugout to get ready to bat. As Adam made his way off the field, he looked to the bleachers. Sapphie was seated daintily on Courtney's lap. She had a red scarf tied around her neck. Mr. and Mrs. Hollinger waved to Adam. Zeph was seated on the ground, licking Arabella's hand. Adam shuddered.

In the dugout, Adam's hands were still shaking.

"What's wrong with you?" Patrick asked. "You did great."

"It's Belle," Adam said. "Maybe she *is* a witch. As soon as I saw her, I couldn't pitch fast anymore."

"You think she put a spell on you?" Patrick asked.

"I don't know what to think," Adam said. "And now Zeph is there, licking her hand like she's a friend."

"Maybe she is." Patrick shrugged.

"Patrick," Coach Harris called. "Adam, Steve, Alex. Warm up!"

The first four batters left the dugout to warm up. Alex, the star batter, swung three bats to limber up his arms. Patrick and Steve both used two. Adam used only one. As he swung at the air, he kept stealing glances at Belle. Every time he looked over, Belle smiled and waved. Why was she always looking at him? Courtney was busy with her text messages. Mr. and Mrs. Hollinger were occupied with the puppies. Why was Belle the only one staring at Adam?

Adam watched her mouth carefully. Either she was chewing gum, or she was... What? Was she chanting something?

Adam shuddered and promised himself he'd stop looking at her.

Before Patrick went to bat, Coach Harris called the team to the dugout. "Remember," he said softly, "York has a weak infield. If you can hit balls there, you have a better chance of getting on base."

The team cheered. "1-2-3-Reds!"

"Three up, three down," the York players cheered as Patrick went to bat. York's pitcher was fast. Patrick swung at the first pitch but missed.

"Stee-rike!" the umpire called.

"That's okay, Patrick," Alex called. "That was just practice."

The next pitch was an obvious ball.

"One and one," the ump called.

"This time," Alex called out.

On the third pitch, Patrick shifted his weight to his back leg, firmly planted in the batter's box like he was going to hit a homer. But when the ball got to the plate, Patrick laid down a perfect bunt that dribbled lazily between third base and the plate.

The White Sox screamed. Patrick made it safely to first by the time the catcher fumbled for the ball. Flustered, he overthrew, allowing Patrick to take second.

"Go Reds," Mr. Hollinger called from the stands.

Adam looked over. His parents were cheering.
Courtney was texting someone. Arabella now had
Zeph on her lap and was waving a red scarf in the
air, shouting "Let's go Reds!"

Adam shuddered to think of Zeph so close to
her.

"You're up, Adam," Coach Harris called.
"Wait for your pitch." Coach Harris pulled his ear to
remind Adam to aim for the infield.

Adam took one last look at the bleachers.
Courtney was busy texting, and he saw Mrs. Hollinger
poke her shoulder and point to Adam. Begrudgingly,
Courtney put away her phone and watched her
brother. Mr. Hollinger was on the edge of his seat,
the camera poised and ready to capture Adam's performance. Next to them, Belle was patting Zeph,
who was still seated on her lap, and Sapphie was
seated on the bleacher next to her. Again, her
mouth seemed to be moving. Adam squinted to try
to determine whether she was chewing gum, or
whether she was chanting.

"Hollinger," Coach Harris yelled.

Adam snapped out of it and took his place at
the plate.

The first pitch seemed to come out of nowhere. Adam took a swing, but his bat was miles
away from making contact.

"Take your time, Hollinger," Coach Harris
yelled. "Pick your pitch."

Adam nodded. He looked the pitcher in the
eye. The pitcher snarled and threw again.

This time, Adam made contact, but it was a
foul. It landed over near the stands. Sapphie jumped
down from her seat and tried to chase the ball.
Luckily, Belle had hold of her leash. Adam turned to

watch the commotion, and Belle made eye contact with him, waving.

"Oh and two, the count," the umpire called.

Adam swallowed hard.

The next pitch was perfect. Adam took a hard swing at it, but his aim was too low, and he just skimmed the ball. It popped out toward left field. Adam's heart pounded. He watched the ball out of the corner of his eye and dashed to first base, but the left fielder easily caught it. Adam skidded to a halt halfway to first base while the crowd applauded for the Sox. Adam felt terrible, causing an out for his team.

"That's all right, Hollinger," Coach Harris yelled. "You'll get 'em at the mound!" He turned to Steve. "You're up, Steve-O! Go get 'em."

Steve was a strong hitter, and Adam watched, hoping Steve would bring Patrick home. The first pitch was a perfect strike, but Steve didn't even swing. He only swung at pitches he liked. He let the next two pitches go by—both were balls. Finally, Steve took a swing at the fourth pitch, and he hit a line-drive right between the shortstop and the second baseman. He got safely to first. Meanwhile, Patrick made it to third, and it looked like he was going to try for home.

The White Sox were shouting. "Throw home! Throw home!"

To distract them, Steve ran to second base. Since Steve was closer to the player with the ball, the player ran to second base to tag Steve out. Still, Steve's distraction allowed Alex to run home.

The Reds shouted.

"One, nothing," Coach Harris shouted. "Here we go!"

Alex stepped to the plate. He was the team's power hitter.

"I see one run waiting on third base," Coach Harris called to him. "And the other run is swinging a bat at home!"

"Swing, swing, swing!" the team shouted. "Knock a homer!"

Alex stood like a hero, looking more like a seventh grader than a fifth grader. He nodded confidently at the pitcher.

"Wait for your pitch," Coach Harris warned.

But Alex liked to swing at everything, and he usually hit it, too. The first pitch was a little high, but he swung anyway. Patrick ran toward home, and Alex took to the field.

"There are two outs. Run!"

Alex flew down the bases. Adam screamed along with the rest of the Reds. But the White Sox's outfield was one of the best in the league, and the right fielder snatched the ball out of the air, leaping up as if the laws of gravity did not apply to him.

"Great catch," York's coach called. "Bring it in, boys." The York players hustled to their dugout.

"Great catch, York," Coach Harris called. "Reds, we'll get 'em next inning."

While the boys took their places on the field, Coach Harris called Adam to the side along the trees behind the dugout.

"What happened out there at bat? You've got to focus," he told Adam.

"I know. I got distracted."

Coach Harris shook his head. "This is an important game."

"I know," Adam said.

"What's distracting you?" Coach asked. "When you're up at bat, you've got to watch the pitcher and the field."

"I'm sorry, I..." Adam's voice trailed off. He couldn't tell Coach Harris he'd been distracted by a witch.

"*I* know what distracted him," Courtney said snidely. She was standing right behind Adam, and Belle was with her. "Adam has a crush on Belle. Every time he looks at her, his ears turn red, and he messes up."

"I do not," Adam said.

"I think he does," Courtney told Coach Harris. "Look how red his ears are turning right now."

Coach looked skeptically at Belle.

"I'll take care of this," Belle said.

"Just do it quickly," Coach said. "We're taking the field. You girls shouldn't even be back here."

Coach walked away to offer encouragement to the rest of the team.

"Adam," Belle said.

"I *don't* have a crush on you," Adam said angrily.

"Okay, okay. But listen. Whether or not you do," she said.

"I don't," Adam insisted. "Courtney, you're so stupid. You're always spreading lies about me—just because you think I'm going to tell Mom and Dad about JJ."

"Who's JJ?" Belle asked.

"No one," Courtney said quickly. "In fact, I have to go. Meghan's coming, and we're going to do something fun instead of watch you play badly." She ran off toward the bleachers, checking her cell phone.

Adam rolled his eyes.

"Reds, we need a pitcher," the umpire called from the field.

"Look," Belle said. "Don't worry about your sister. You need to concentrate on your game. In fact, I've got something that will help you." Belle reached behind her neck and untied a red, satiny ribbon. Hanging from the ribbon was a large red ruby. "It's an amulet. It's red like your team and will bring you good luck. It'll help you focus your energies. Wear it around your neck during the game."

Adam's ears turned red as Belle tied the ribbon around his neck. He looked at the amulet. It was a deep red that caught the light of the sun.

"Hollinger, let's go," Coach called.

Adam nodded at Belle, tucked the ruby under his jersey, and hit the field.

"What was that about?" Patrick asked as he tossed a warm-up to Adam.

Adam shrugged.

"Witch," Patrick mouthed before running back to second base.

The umpire called for the inning to start. Once again, all eyes were on Adam. He took a deep breath. He felt the amulet against his skin. It was growing warm with his body heat.

She can't really *be a witch,* Adam thought. *Can she?*

He focused on the amulet and threw a perfect breaking ball.

"Great pitch," came shouts from the bleachers—even parents from York.

Adam smiled. Instead of looking into the stands, he focused on the ruby. He felt a new wave of confidence, throwing strike after strike. When the other team managed to hit one of his pitches, the Reds were there to field the hits. If Adam could just keep this up, it would be an easy win.

~ NINETEEN ~
Disappearing Act

The puppies stayed behind while Courtney left to meet Meghan. Mr. and Mrs. Hollinger held their leashes, but they were too focused on the game to pay much attention to the puppies, and before long Zeph and Sapphie had crawled under the bleachers.

"Where did that nice lady go?" Sapphie asked. She bent down on to lap up some soda that had spilled.

"You shouldn't drink that," Zeph said.

"Why not?"

"Because our people didn't give it to us. We're only supposed to eat what they give us."

"Nonsense," Sapphie said. She barked, but no one heard her above the din of the cheering crowd. "See?" she said. "If they're too busy to pay attention to someone as cute as *me*, then why should I worry about what they think?" She turned to stare her brother in the eye. "Try some," she said.

"Well," Zeph said. "It does smell pretty interesting."

"It tastes even better," she said.

Zeph licked the soda. "Actually, it *does* taste pretty good."

"See?" Sapphie said. "You should listen to me more often."

Further down the bleachers, a small boy dropped a bag of popcorn.

"Mine, mine, *mine*!" Sapphie called. She pulled her leash as tight as it would go. She could only reach a few pieces of popcorn, but the salty, buttery taste was well worth the effort.

Zeph shook his head. "You'll be sick later."

"No, I won't." Sapphie finished her popcorn. "Anyway, where did Courtney go? She was letting me sit on the bleachers with her. And how do you like my new scarf?" Sapphie twirled around to model the scarf for Zeph. "When Courtney left, we had to sit on the ground. Now no one can see my scarf."

"I don't think dogs are supposed to sit on bleachers," Zeph said.

"Well, the scarf lady said we could..."

"Her name is Arabella," Zeph reminded his sister. "Belle for short."

"Fine. Belle said we could. And so did Courtney."

"Where is Courtney?" Zeph asked.

"Not sure," Sapphie said. "She told me she was going off to meet someone named Meghan and that they were going to go make their hair look pretty. I don't know why they didn't take me along."

"That sounds strange," Zeph said.

"I know, I know, *I know*! I'm a princess, and if anyone's hair needs to look pretty, it's mine," Sapphie said.

"Did she mention anything about JJ?" Zeph asked.

"That's all she *ever* mentions," Sapphie said. "What is a *JJ*, anyway?"

"JJ is that boy who was at our house the other day. I don't like the smell of him."

"Oh, *that* JJ," Sapphie remembered. "I don't like him very much, either. He's always stealing Courtney's attention away from me."

"Is Arabella going to see JJ too?"

"I don't know," Sapphie said. "Maybe. Why?"

"Just something Adam's been saying. If Arabella and JJ are friends, maybe Arabella really *is* a witch. Did you see the thing she put on Adam?"

"That pretty red thing?" Sapphie asked. "I'd like to wear that on my collar. You think Adam would give it to me?"

Zeph ignored her. "Have you noticed that ever since she gave Adam that red thing, the crowd has been cheering more loudly than before?"

Sapphie was too busy trying to reach a soft pretzel that had fallen through the bleachers. "What were you saying?"

"Never mind, Sapphie. I only wish I weren't stuck on this leash so I could go see what Courtney's up to."

Sapphie barked indignantly. "I'm only stuck on the leash because I'm trying to be good."

"Since when do you ever try to be good?"

"I thought I'd give it a try today," Sapphie said. "It's not nearly as fun as being bad."

She gave her brother a mischievous look, and he watched as she twisted her body. Her neck easily slipped out of her collar. With a single, shrill bark, she dashed to the soft pretzel, devoured it, and ran off behind the bleachers toward the restrooms.

Zeph went crazy, barking and pulling on his leash until Mr. Hollinger noticed. "Zeph, be quiet," he scolded, until he peeked under the bleacher to see that where Sapphie used to be was now just an empty collar attached to her leash.

~ TWENTY ~
Blue Hair in the Bathroom

Following Courtney's scent, Sapphie wandered down a sidewalk. There were new smells everywhere, and it was difficult to focus. Everywhere she went, people stopped to look at her.

"What are *they* looking at?" she asked herself. "Probably haven't ever seen such a cute dog before with such a cute scarf."

"Did you see that dog?" A woman asked her husband. "She has no collar. I wonder if the poor thing is lost."

Sapphie ignored them. She caught the faint scent of Courtney and followed it. She sniffed and sniffed until she came to a closed door that had a strange symbol on the front. Sapphie sat at the door and barked. At home, if she encountered a closed door, all she had to do was sit and bark, and the door was opened.

"This one is broken," she told herself. "It won't open."

But just as she was about to give up, the door opened, and an elderly woman exited. "Oh my!" the woman said, looking at Sapphie. She held the door open, bewildered, as the little puppy pranced inside.

When Sapphie entered the bathroom, she barked with excitement. There were delightful smells coming from all over. Even better, her bark seemed to bounce off the walls. Sapphie ran about, panting and barking and skittering on the tile floor. She took a turn a little too quickly and skidded into someone's leg. Sapphie shook her head, dazed, but a familiar smell excited her. She looked up to see that the leg she bumped belonged to Courtney, who was too busy leaning over the bathroom sink to notice.

"I sure hope JJ likes my blue hair," Courtney was saying.

Sapphie wagged her tail and barked.

"Courtney, isn't that your dog?" asked Meghan, who stood right next to Courtney.

Courtney looked down. Her hair was pulled over her face, and part of it was wrapped in foil. Sapphie barked happily. She loved the crinkly sound it made and the salty way it tasted when she chewed it. She wagged her tail, remembering that Zeph was terrified of foil. She'd have to tell him about it.

"Sapphie?" Courtney yelled. "What are you doing in here? Bad girl."

Courtney reached down to grab Sapphie, but Sapphie knew better. She knew that nothing good ever followed the phrase *bad girl*. There was no way she'd let Courtney pick her up while she was using *that* tone of voice.

Sapphie turned around and ran under what appeared to be a little doorway.

"She ran into that bathroom stall," Meghan said.

Just as she finished speaking, a woman screamed from inside the stall. "Get it out," she cried. "There's a dog in here!"

"Sapphie," Courtney screamed. "Get out here this minute."

Inside the stall, Sapphie looked up. She saw a strange woman sitting on a white chair, and boy did she look mad. Sapphie backed up slowly until she was back outside the stall.

"The nerve of some pet owners," the woman screeched from the stall. "I'm calling animal control." She opened the stall door. Her hair was fluffy, white, and disheveled. She wore a black sweater and a white scarf and carried a white York flag. She didn't look happy.

"I'm sorry," Meghan muttered. "We..."

"Hmph," the woman insisted. "It would figure the dog is wearing a red scarf and no collar. That's something only ruffians from Lancaster would do."

"Let's get out of here," Meghan suggested.

"I'm with you," Courtney agreed. She grabbed Sapphie, and the two girls ran out of the bathroom toward the baseball field.

"What'll we do?" Meghan asked. "You think she's really going to tell on us?"

"It wasn't our fault. My parents were supposed to be watching Sapphie."

"I don't know if they'll see it that way, Courtney," Meghan said.

The girls turned around. They saw the woman with the black sweater slowly but steadily making her way toward them.

"What should we do?" Courtney asked. Her hair was still done up in foil, and people were starting to stare.

"Let's just go join your parents. We'll put Sapphie under the bleachers and pretend like we were sitting there watching the game the whole time."

"Okay," Courtney agreed. "But what about my hair?"

Just as they turned toward the bleachers, Mrs. Hollinger spotted them. She looked like she had been searching frantically.

"Girls," she said. "What happened to you? Where's Sapphie?"

"She's right here, Mom," Courtney said.

"Thank goodness. But Courtney, what's in your hair?"

"Nothing," Courtney said.

"Nothing? It looks like foil to me. Are you coloring your hair?"

"Umm..." Courtney's cell phone buzzed. She reached into her pocket to pick it up, but Mrs. Hollinger stopped her.

"Don't you dare answer that phone, young lady. I asked you a question and I expect an answer. What happened to your hair? So help me, I'll take away your phone privileges again."

"Fine," Courtney said. She had to fight hard against the urge to check her cell phone. "I was dyeing my hair."

"I never gave you permission to dye your hair," Mrs. Hollinger said.

"Um, I think maybe I should go now," Meghan said.

Mrs. Hollinger took one look at Meghan's hair, which had bright red streaks in it. "Does your mother know you dyed your hair, Meghan?"

Meghan shrugged. "She doesn't care."

"Well I do," Mrs. Hollinger said. "Courtney, if you want to do something like dye your hair, you have to ask us. You can't just do whatever you want. You're only in middle school."

"That's dumb," Courtney said. "I'm in seventh grade now. You're treating me like a baby. What's wrong with dyeing my hair?"

Mrs. Hollinger put her hands on her hips. "You wait until your father sees what you've done. What color is your hair under those foils? Is it as red as Meghan's?"

"No," Courtney said.

Mrs. Hollinger breathed a sigh of relief.

"It's blue," Courtney said with a smirk.

Mrs. Hollinger opened her mouth to scold her daughter, but she was interrupted by an older woman in a black sweater.

"Is this your daughter?" the woman asked angrily.

"Yes," Mrs. Hollinger said.

"I've got a complaint about your daughter. And her dog. That dog came right into the stall while I was in the bathroom stall."

Mrs. Hollinger blushed. "I'm so sorry," she said.

"And when I went to confront your daughter about it, she ran off like a banshee was chasing her. As if I wouldn't be able to recognize her with crazy hair like that."

"I'm sorry," Mrs. Hollinger said. "I'm sure she was just excited about the game. Our dog got loose. Broke right out of her collar. We were worried sick," Mrs. Hollinger explained.

"That's none of my concern. I think it's a terrible thing when an old woman can't even use the restroom in peace. And I'll bet you're all rooting for the Reds, aren't you? It figures. Reds fans." She threw her arms in the air with disgust.

A man passing by, who was wearing a Lancaster Reds shirt, overheard the old woman's remark.

"Hey, lady," he shouted. "You'd better watch who you insult. The Reds fans are better than York's fans any day. And we're sure kicking your butt in this game."

"How rude," the old woman huffed.

Just then, Mr. Hollinger approached with Zeph. He was carrying Sapphie's empty leash. "Good," he said. "You found her."

Mrs. Hollinger frowned.

"What's wrong?" Mr. Hollinger asked.

"This old lady here was just insulting us Reds fans," the man in the Reds shirt told Mr. Hollinger.

"And your daughter," the old woman told Mr. Hollinger, "is an irresponsible punk."

Mr. Hollinger took a deep breath. "I'm not sure what's going on here, but from the looks of it, Courtney is partly to blame. I don't want to start any riots here. How about this?" he asked the old woman. "I'll work things out with my daughter at home. I'll make sure she gets a good talking to. But for now, let's just all get back to the game." He turned to his wife. "Adam pitched a no-hitter for two innings in a row."

"Oh no," Mrs. Hollinger said. "I'm sorry I missed it."

The old woman huffed. "So your son's the one who's striking out all our White Sox? It figures." She dismissed it all with the flick of her hand and trudged off to the bleachers.

Courtney raised one eyebrow and looked at her father.

"Courtney," Mr. Hollinger said. "Don't think I don't see your hair. I don't want to miss Adam pitch, but we'll discuss this when we get home. There better be no other disruptions today."

Mr. Hollinger turned and headed to the bleachers. Zeph, Sapphie, and Mrs. Hollinger followed, leaving Courtney and Meghan by themselves.

"Might as well finish my hair," Courtney said. "I'm already in trouble."

Meghan nodded. The two girls went back toward the bathrooms, hurrying to make sure the Hollingers didn't see them.

"That Meghan," Mrs. Hollinger said to her husband. "She seems like a bad influence on Courtney."

"Yeah," agreed Mr. Hollinger, taking his seat on the bleachers next to Belle.

The Reds were at bat, and Adam sat, enjoying a well-deserved break on the bench. It was the fifth inning, and it looked like his arm was starting to ache.

"I remember being that age," Belle said. "Maybe I could talk to her."

"That's a good idea," Mrs. Hollinger said. "I feel like whenever I give her advice, she wants to do the exact opposite. Maybe someone closer to her own age would get through to her."

"Teenagers," Mr. Hollinger sighed.

"Courtney isn't even thirteen yet," Mrs. Hollinger reminded him.

"She acts like it," he said.

"Maybe you *should* talk to her, Belle. She's probably back in the bathroom."

Mr. Hollinger chuckled. "You already worked your magic on Adam. Whatever you said to him sure gave him his confidence back."

Belle smiled. "I'm just good with kids," she said. "Excuse me." She stepped over the bench and headed toward the bathroom.

As she left, the sun hid behind a cloud.

"Brrr," Mrs. Hollinger said. "The weather sure is getting cooler." She put on jacket. "I just hope Courtney's not too cold—wherever she ran off to. All she's wearing is an old t-shirt."

~ * ~

In the meantime, Zeph and Sapphie had situated themselves back under the bleachers. Sapphie's collar was back on, tighter than ever.

"This is bad, bad, *bad*!" Sapphie said, scratching at her collar with her hind leg.

"Well, what did you expect?" Zeph asked without sympathy. "I *told* you, you can't go running off whenever you feel like it."

"Hmph," Sapphie said. "You're no fun, and neither are they."

"Where did you go?" Zeph asked.

"I found my Courtney. She was in this great place with lots of smells, and this smelly old woman sitting on a white—"

Zeph sighed. "You've been missing a good game. Everyone's been cheering for Adam. I wonder if it has anything to do with—"

"Hey you two," Mr. Hollinger called, peeking down through the bleachers. "No escaping again, okay?"

Just as he spoke, someone dropped a hot dog, and Sapphie and Zeph forgot their conversation. They had a quiet feast while the crowd cheered for Adam as he and the Reds finished a victorious game.

~ TWENTY-ONE ~
An Icy Victory

"We need to celebrate," Mr. Hollinger said, snapping a few shots of Adam from the other side of the fence. The Reds won 7-2, and Adam had done much of the work with his pitching.

"Yeah," Adam agreed.

"Let's go to Carlton's Comics. You can buy any comic book you want."

Adam smiled.

"Hey Adam," Patrick called. "Come on."

Adam ran to join his team on the pitcher's mound.

"Normally," Patrick said after Adam arrived, "we dump the water cooler on our coach."

Coach Harris, who stood at the center of the mound, smiled nervously.

"But this time," Patrick said, "we thought we should dump it on our MVP, too!"

Adam's teammates pushed him next to Coach Harris. All Adam saw was an ocean of smiling faces, and he felt the cool rush of ice water on his face.

"Ahhgg," he screamed.

"Brrr," Coach added.

When the icy shower was finished, Coach Harris laughed and patted Adam on the shoulder. His hand splashed ice water all over Adam and his teammates. "Nice job, Hollinger. I knew you could do it."

Adam tried to give everyone a hug to get his team as wet as possible while they all laughed and cheered. All around, people were snapping pictures.

After a few minutes, the boys calmed down.

"We should all be proud of the way we played," Coach said. "We'll have practice again next week, and we'll talk about the next game, and, hopefully, our final rivals."

"The Altoona Angels," Alex said with awe.

"No one ever beats them," Steve said.

"Now boys," Coach Harris said. "Let's not ruin the day with any fears about the future. We did an *awesome* job today. Time to celebrate. I say it's time for... pizza. On me."

Everyone cheered.

Mr. and Mrs. Hollinger snapped a picture. "Adam, you're soaked," they said.

"It's okay," Adam explained. "It feels good to win."

"Well, you did good," Mr. Hollinger said.

"You did *well*," Mrs. Hollinger corrected. "We're proud of you."

"Thanks," Adam said.

A family dressed in York colors heading to the parking lot but changed direction and walked toward Adam.

"Son," the man said to Adam. "I just wanted to congratulate you on your pitching." He held out his hand—his arm decorated with a white York sweatshirt—for a handshake. "You've got quite a future ahead of you. You'll be a high-school star, and I can just see colleges fighting over you."

Despite the cold water, Adam felt his face warm and blush. "Th-thanks," he said, shaking hands.

The man's son, a player from the York White Sox, extended his hand as well. "Good pitching," he said. "You guys deserved to win. Just promise you'll represent us well against the last two teams. You guys'll make it to the final game, I just know it."

Adam smiled.

"Of course we will," Coach Harris said, chomping on his gum. "You Sox played a great game, too."

The York player smiled, waved, and headed back to the car with his family.

"That man was right, Adam," Mrs. Hollinger said. "You should be proud of the way you pitched."

Adam nodded.

"I invited the team for pizza," Coach Harris said. "We're going to Angelo's. I hope our star pitcher will be able to join us?"

"Fine with me," Mr. Hollinger said. "But we'll have to stop home first. We've got the dogs, and..." He looked around. "We've got to find Courtney." He squinted, and Adam could tell he was getting angry. "We're going to have to start keeping a tighter leash on her."

"Adam can ride with me," Coach Harris said. "There's always room for Patrick's best friend. And you can join us when you're able. Good luck finding Courtney."

Adam bent down to say bye to Zeph. As he did, he saw Belle and Courtney emerge from a wooded area behind the field. Half of Courtney's hair was now streaked with blue dye. She looked down, covering her face with her blue hair. Belle put an arm on Courtney's shoulder and walked her over to the bleachers.

"I'd better go talk to her," Mrs. Hollinger said, sighing.

"Good grief, her hair," Mr. Hollinger added. "And what jacket is she wearing?"

Mrs. Hollinger turned to look. Courtney wore a blue jean jacket made of distressed fabric. Its collar was turned up, and it was way too big on her.

"Now I may be wrong," Mr. Hollinger said, "but that jacket looks like it belongs to a *boy*."

"Hmm," Mrs. Hollinger said, handing Adam a dry sweatshirt. "Why don't you go ahead with Patrick and Coach Harris? You just enjoy yourself. I think we're overdue for long talk with your sister. Hopefully, we'll see you at the pizza place later on."

Adam nodded. "Darn," he whispered to Patrick from inside Coach Harris's truck. "I would have liked to see Courtney finally get in trouble. It happens once in a blue moon."

The wind in Adam's hair felt great as Coach Harris circled the parking lot. It felt even better as he watched Courtney get into the back of his parents' minivan, her arms crossed against their disapproving looks.

~ TWENTY-TWO ~
A Broken Promise

"So Adam," Patrick asked during the pizza party. "You pitched an amazing game. How did you do it?"

The boys had eaten slice after slice of delicious pizza. Everyone was now full and tired, and the celebration was winding down.

Adam shook his head. "I'm not sure." He took off the red necklace Belle had given him and held it out for Patrick to see. "Arabella Spinelli gave me this," he said.

"You think it's magic?" Patrick asked.

"I don't know." Adam shrugged. "Every time I got distracted by something, I just focused on the necklace, and it helped me concentrate on pitching."

"Hmm," Patrick said. "We'll have to investigate further. Riley Couth would *definitely* think that's suspicious. When's the next time you're raking leaves for Arabella?"

"Tomorrow," Adam sighed.

"I can't make it tomorrow," Patrick said. "I'm visiting my mom's family. Maybe you could do some spy work for me."

"Spy work?"

"Yeah," Patrick said. "Try to get invited inside. Then snoop around. Maybe you'll uncover something. You know, gather clues like Riley Couth. Look for evidence."

"I don't want to be inside her house. Especially not without you," Adam insisted. "What if she really *is* a witch? Riley Couth never had to deal with magic. What if she really *can* turn me into a toad?"

"Who can turn you into a toad?" asked Mr. Hollinger, who had just arrived.

"No one, Dad," Adam lied. "We were just talking about... um..."

"A movie," Patrick blurted.

"What movie?" Mr. Hollinger asked.

Adam felt his ears turning red.

"There he is," Coach Harris said. "There's the father of the star pitcher."

Adam was glad for the distraction. He took the red necklace from Patrick and shoved it in his pocket. "I'll keep you posted on what I find out," Adam whispered while his dad talked to the coach. "But I'm not promising anything."

~ * ~

Mr. Hollinger had come alone, and Adam sat in the front seat during the drive home.

"Sorry I missed the pizza dinner, sport," he said. "We had to give Courtney a talking to." Mr. Hollinger kept looking over at Adam and it was making him nervous.

"Adam?" Mr. Hollinger asked finally.

"Yes?"

"You haven't noticed Courtney spending time with anyone she shouldn't be? A boy? Someone older, maybe?"

Adam swallowed hard. He promised Courtney he wouldn't say anything. Besides, as long as Adam kept Courtney's secret, she had to be nice to him. He didn't want things to go back to the way they were, with Courtney tormenting him all the time.

"I've been pretty busy with practice all the time," Adam said. "And raking leaves," he added. "You know Courtney doesn't ever tell me anything."

Mr. Hollinger nodded. "I know Belle really appreciates all the work you've done in her backyard. She told me so during the game today."

"Hmm," Adam said.

"What's wrong?" Mr. Hollinger asked.

"Nothing," Adam said. Although he wanted to tell his dad all about his suspicions, he knew he shouldn't.

They drove past a store that was decorated for Halloween. "Do you believe in witches?" Adam asked, eyeing a light-up display of a green-faced witch riding a broomstick above a pumpkin patch of glowing jack-o-lanterns.

"Real witches?" Mr. Hollinger asked, laughing. "No, I don't think so. I did when I was a kid, though. They scared me silly." He looked at Adam. "Why do you ask?"

"Just curious," Adam said. "Never mind." He looked out the window. "This isn't the way home," Adam said.

Mr. Hollinger smiled. "Did you forget already? I thought we'd stop at your favorite comic store."

Adam smiled. He'd forgotten all about his father's promise to buy him a comic book. All his worries about witches and high-school kids melted away. He couldn't have been happier. He had helped his team win the game, his sister was finally getting in trouble, and he was spending time alone with his dad. Adam was so happy about winning that he felt like he was walking on clouds all the way into the store.

"Can I help you?" a voice asked as soon as Adam entered the comic shop.

"I'm looking for the newest Logan Zephyr comic book," Adam said proudly. "It's about a space sorceress..."

"Well then, you must be celebrating something special," the voice behind the counter said. "Like winning a baseball game."

"What?" Adam asked. He peered across the counter at the clerk who was bent down over some boxes. When he saw who it was, he felt like he was sinking into a pit. It was Arabella Spinelli, and she was wearing a Carlton's Comics uniform.

"Belle?" Adam asked.

"Great game," she said. "I didn't get to congratulate you. You were surrounded by all your fans, and I had to get to work."

"What are you doing here?" Adam asked, ignoring her congratulations.

"I work here," she said.

"You work *here*?"

Arabella nodded. "I needed a part-time job. Something to pay the bills while I finish school."

Adam swallowed hard. Never in a million years would he have expected to find Belle working at the comic shop. For once in his life, he wished he had a cell phone. He couldn't wait to tell Patrick.

"Belle," Mr. Hollinger said, finally entering the store. "Long time, no see. Didn't realize you had to work today. Nice of you to spend your time off at Adam's game."

"You knew she worked here?" Adam asked. "Why didn't you tell me?"

"I didn't think it mattered," Mr. Hollinger said.

"Well, it does," Adam insisted.

"Why?" Mr. Hollinger asked.

"It just does, Dad."

"Okay, well now you know." Mr. Hollinger eyed Adam suspiciously. "You okay, Adam?"

"I guess," Adam said.

"Okay, do you know which comic book you want?"

Belle smiled. "He does. He chose the newest adventure of Logan Zephyr. I started reading it this afternoon. It's a great story. In this one, Logan goes to a planet ruled by a space sorceress. But I don't want to spoil it for Adam."

"What would you know about it?" Adam muttered under his breath, not daring to say it loud enough for her to hear.

"Say, Belle," Mr. Hollinger said. "Whatever you said to Adam really helped him at the game today."

"Oh, it wasn't what I said," Belle explained. "It was the special Reds amulet." She smiled. "It brought him good luck. You can keep it, Adam," she said.

"Ah," Mr. Hollinger said. "A good luck charm. I remember having a good luck charm when I played football in high school. It was this keychain my grandfather gave me. It had a red oak leaf on it and was so worn out because I insisted on hanging it around my neck the entire football season. I wouldn't take it off for anything. I showered with it on, slept with it on..." Mr. Hollinger lost himself in memories.

"Are you still wearing the amulet?" Belle asked.

Adam's ears turned red. "It's in my pocket," he muttered.

"Let me see it," Belle said.

Miserably, Adam handed her the amulet.

"It matches your uniform," Mr. Hollinger said.

Belle placed the ribbon over Adam's head. "Keep it on," she said. "Keep it safe for the rest of the season."

"It looks sharp," Mr. Hollinger added.

"It does," Belle agreed.

Adam's ears matched the color of the red amulet as Belle handed him a copy of *Logan Zephyr and the Space Sorceress*.

Adam took the comic book. "Thanks, Dad," he said. "I guess I'd better get to the car and start reading." He headed quickly for the door.

"Adam, wait," Belle called. "Are you still coming over tomorrow to finish raking leaves?"

Adam didn't say anything. His arm ached, and after seeing Belle at his favorite comic book store, the last thing he wanted to do was rake leaves.

But before Adam could think of an excuse, Mr. Hollinger answered for him. "Of course he'll be over. Say around eleven?"

"That's great," Belle said. "See you then."

In the car, Mr. Hollinger looked at Adam with a smile. "Your first crush, huh?"

"What?" Adam said.

"Courtney told us you have a crush on her. It's okay. It's normal for boys to have crushes..."

"Dad!" Adam protested. "I don't have a crush on her." He could feel his ears turning bright red—perhaps even purple.

"It's okay, Adam," Mr. Hollinger said. "I won't tell anyone. I had a crush on lots of girls in my years.

Is that why you don't want to rake leaves at her house?"

"You've got it all wrong, Dad," Adam insisted. "Courtney's a liar."

"I know Courtney's difficult to deal with sometimes," Mr. Hollinger said, "but don't be mean."

"I'm not being mean," Adam said. "I'm just telling the truth. Courtney *is* a liar." Adam was so angry. He had been working hard to keep Courtney's secret for her, and here she was being as mean as ever, spreading lies about him just like she always did.

"I don't think she's a liar," Mr. Hollinger said. "She's going through a phase, yes. But a liar? I don't think so."

Adam scowled. He spoke without thinking. "I'm not supposed to tell you this," Adam said angrily, "but she's been hanging around with a guy named JJ for a while now. He's in high school, and he's being a bad influence on her. JJ and his friends are always so mean to me."

The smile on Mr. Hollinger's face faded, and he slowed his car. "How long has she been hanging out with JJ?"

"For a while," Adam said. "She lied to you about JJ and lied to you about me having a crush." Adam's anger faded as he considered the consequence of tattling on his sister. "Please don't tell her I told you. She made me promise not to tell and said she'd be nice to me as long as I kept her secret."

"Really?" Mr. Hollinger asked.

Adam nodded. "But now that she's spreading lies about me, I don't see how it matters anymore.

Still, don't tell her I told you," Adam pleaded. "She'll be so mad. And so will JJ."

Mr. Hollinger squinted.

Adam gulped. "Am I in trouble?"

He sighed. "It wasn't right of you to lie to me. I'm your father."

"Sorry, Dad. I guess you'll probably be taking away my comic book..."

Mr. Hollinger shook his head. "No, Adam. You earned that. You pitched a good game. And I know how Courtney can be sometimes. I know you didn't want to keep her secret, right?"

Adam nodded, but he couldn't help thinking that he *enjoyed* having the secret because it forced Courtney to be nice to him.

"I won't tell her I heard it from you," Mr. Hollinger assured him. "But you did the right thing telling me."

The rest of the drive home, Mr. Hollinger held the steering wheel tightly. He spoke a little about the game, but mostly he was silent, staring at the road with a frown.

When he got home, Adam went right to his room with Zeph. No matter what his dad promised, Courtney would know that Adam told her secret. And when JJ found out, there was no telling what he would do for revenge. Whatever his parents said to Courtney, Adam didn't want to know about it. It would just make him worry about the ways she'd try to get even with him.

He leaned back against his pillow and tried to relax. Finally, with Zeph curled at his feet, he opened his comic book and read *Logan Zephyr and the Space Sorceress.*

~ TWENTY-THREE ~
A Frightening Folder and an Empty Bag of Leaves

On Sunday morning, Adam trudged down the stairs for breakfast. He wasn't looking forward to raking leaves for Belle—especially after reading all about the space sorceress, who liked to wear strange clothing, just like Arabella and Cassandra. She wore a million pieces of jewelry, each one with a special power. She mixed together potions using strange herbs from her planet. One of the potions even looked like it was the same color as Belle's mulled apple cider. And in one of the scenes, the space sorceress turned one of Logan Zephyr's crew members into a sea slug. If Riley Couth were on the case, he would definitely be suspicious.

Adam shivered. "Where's Courtney?" he asked at the breakfast table to put his mind on something else.

"She's grounded for the day," Mr. Hollinger explained. "And that includes no cell phone." He took Courtney's cell phone out of his pocket to illustrate his point.

"She's grounded to the house," Mrs. Hollinger explained. "She's welcome to eat with us, as I told her. But she refuses to come out of her room. You know how she gets..." Mrs. Hollinger turned away and sniffed away the threat of a tear.

"Adam," Mr. Hollinger said quietly. "We need you to tell us if she's making any plans to hang out with this JJ character."

"I don't like being a tattle-tale," Adam said. "Courtney gets mad, and then she spreads lies about me through Marnie. Everyone *still* thinks I have a

crush on Ms. Wilkerson, which I don't," Adam insisted. "And *you* thought I had a crush on Arabella Spinelli. Yuk." Adam already felt his ears getting red.

Mr. Hollinger said, "Courtney's your sister.
You shouldn't feel afraid of her. And it's always best
if you tell us things."

Adam nodded, even though he wasn't sure he
agreed.

~ * ~

While the three people ate, Zeph and Sapphie
sat underneath the table. They knew they weren't
supposed to beg for food, but every once in a while
a tasty scrap managed to fall to the floor, and they
were quick to scoop it up.

"Did you hear that?" Sapphie asked Zeph beneath the table.

"Hear what?"

"That your Adam's going to tattle-tale on my
Courtney."

"He's just trying to keep her out of trouble,"
Zeph said.

"Well, he's about to get her *into* trouble.
She'll get him back," Sapphie growled.

"What?"

"I overheard Courtney talking to JJ at the
game yesterday. They've got the best Halloween
plan. They're going to scare Adam out of his skin."

Zeph growled. "You'd better tell me, Sapphie."

"Why should I?"

"Because it's my job to protect my Adam. If
something bad is going to happen to him, I'd like to
know about it."

"Maybe if you weren't so boring, I'd tell you.
It's no fun to always follow the rules."

"Maybe if you and Courtney followed the rules more often, you two wouldn't be in so much trouble all the time."

Sapphie scratched her collar and growled. "My collar *is* pretty tight."

"Well that's what you get for disobeying," Zeph said. "Tell me about JJ's Halloween prank?"

"All I can say is that it's on Halloween, when Adam and his friends are out trick-or-treating. Whatever that means. I'm not sure what else they were talking about. People are confusing sometimes. And besides, they were ignoring me."

Zeph growled again. "I'll be sure to go with Adam, then, on this *trick-or-treat* thing."

"What is it?" Sapphie asked. "Trick-or-treat..."

"*Treats* are yummy," Zeph said, looking up at the corgis' jar of cookies. "But I'm not sure I like the sounds of *tricks*. Still, I'll protect Adam anyway."

"Suit yourself," Sapphie said. "I'm staying home where it's nice and warm."

~ * ~

Up on the table, Adam was just finishing his cantaloupe. "I guess I should get over to Belle's," he said. "And get this raking over with."

"Adam," Mrs. Hollinger said. "It's okay to admit if you have a crush on her."

"Dad!" Adam complained. "I *don't* have a crush on Belle or anyone else, for that matter."

"Okay," Mrs. Hollinger said, though she couldn't help but smile.

Adam wanted to tell them the *real* reason he didn't want to rake her leaves. But how could he explain to them that she was a witch? They would never believe him. He had read his entire comic book last night, cover-to-cover. He had some new clues about witches, and he couldn't wait to discuss them with Patrick. But for now, he'd have to play detective and gather evidence. So he gulped down the rest of his orange juice and headed for the door, grabbing his gray detective hat for good measure.

"Why don't you bring Zeph?" Mr. Hollinger asked. "I'm sure he'd love to help you."

"Okay," Adam said. At least Zeph could help protect him if Belle tried to put a spell on him.

When he got to Belle's back yard, the hair on the back of his neck prickled. The yard was full of leaves. It looked like he hadn't raked at all the last time he was there. He walked to the tree to get the rake, which he had left leaning against it. What he saw behind the tree made him feel sick to his stomach. There was a used paper leaf disposal bag. It looked like it had been used—but it was empty. Had Belle dumped out the leaves Adam raked a few days ago?

"There you are," Belle said, coming out of the house.

Adam jumped.

She wore a long, flowing skirt, as usual. She wore a thick fleece jacket over her shirt and dozens of necklaces, so she looked a little more normal than usual. Still, Adam saw her many rings gleaming in the sunlight. She noticed Adam studying her outfit, so she spun around.

"Like my skirt?" she asked. "It's bright red in honor of your team's victory."

She smiled, but Adam frowned. He didn't care *what* kind of skirt she wore. He just wanted to get the leaves raked and get out of there. He adjusted the rake in his hand.

"There are so many leaves. I'm so glad you could help me out."

Adam cleared his throat. He felt like a cat had gotten his tongue. When he finally felt able to speak again he said, "It looks like I didn't even rake the last time I was here."

Belle laughed nervously. "That's what happens in autumn." She pulled a lawn chair to the edge of the patio and brushed leaves and acorns from the seat. "You don't mind if I sit here while you rake, do you? I have some work to do."

"For school?"

"Yes. And I get so much more done outdoors than indoors. I guess I'm just a nature person."

Adam shuddered. In his *Logan Zephyr* comic book, the Space Sorceress loved the outdoors, too. She lived on a planet made of strange, colorful forests, and she liked doing everything outside.

"Strike one," Adam muttered as he started raking. "Zeph, you stay nearby."

Zeph howled and stayed close to Adam. He wagged his stubbly little tail and chased leaves as they fell from the trees. He gathered his catches, bringing them to Adam.

Out of the corner of his eye, Adam watched as Belle scribbled something in her notebook—that same purple notebook she had before.

"So, I was talking to Courtney yesterday," Belle said after a long silence.

Adam continued raking.

"She dyed her hair a pretty weird blue. Your parents seemed mad."

"She's pretty stupid sometimes," Adam said. "She lies and says dumb things."

Belle shrugged. "Sometimes kids just get that way. Especially in middle school."

"I hope I *never* get that way," Adam said.

"What concerns me more is JJ. I saw him at the game. He looks like a rough character. Besides, what would a tenth grader want with a seventh grader, anyway?"

"I don't know," Adam said. "They're both pretty mean."

"Hmm." Belle jotted something down on her notepad.

Adam thought back to his *Logan Zephyr* comic. The Space Sorceress kept a leather-bound book where she recorded all her spells. She even tried to use one against Logan Zephyr and the crew. Adam shivered as a chill crept up his spine.

"I overheard them talking about Halloween. Do you know if they're making plans?" Belle asked.

"I don't know," Adam said. "I know they're too old to go trick-or-treating. Other than that, she won't tell me anything."

"Hmm," Belle said again.

She didn't say anything after that. She just kept writing in her purple notebook, and Adam was curious about what she was writing. He tried to think straight and be rational, just like Detective Riley Couth. But his mind kept returning to the Space Sorceress and her book of spells.

When he was about halfway done with the yard, his arms ached, and he was already stiff from pitching. He adjusted his detective hat, surveyed the leaf pile, and sighed.

"You need a break," Belle said. "It's rare for a pitcher to stay on the mound the whole game.

Your coach must be proud. You struck out so many batters, it made for quick innings."

Adam pulled his hair over his burning ears.

"Just leave the pile there," Belle said. "You can finish raking the yard some other day. I know you're probably still tired from the game."

Adam nodded.

"Come in for some lemonade. It's home-made."

Adam groaned. He thought about witches' potions. In *Logan Zephyr and the Space Sorceress*, Logan drank a yellow potion and hallucinated for three whole days while the Space Sorceress tried to kidnap the rest of his crew.

"No, thanks," Adam mumbled.

"You've got to be thirsty after raking so much," Belle insisted.

Adam considered for a minute. Patrick would be disappointed if Adam didn't at least go inside to investigate. Maybe he could uncover clues to prove that Belle and Cassandra were witches. Besides, Zeph would be there to protect him. Wouldn't he?

"All right," Adam groaned. "Come on, Zeph."

Zeph was nowhere to be found.

"Zeph?" Adam called. His heart beat faster.

Had Belle put a spell on his dog? Did she turn him into a toad? Adam's mind flashed with horrible memories of last summer when Mr. Frostburg trapped Zeph and Sapphie in his shed. And now Zeph was missing again. Where was he? Adam swallowed hard as the world spun around him. He felt dizzy and sick and—

"Here he is," Belle called, pointing. Zeph had fallen asleep in the leaf pile.

Belle jotted a note in her purple book before leading Adam inside. Adam followed hesitantly, glad to have Zeph for company.

"Have a seat," she told Adam. "I'll go get some lemonade."

Adam sat on the couch while Zeph plopped down at his feet. On the coffee table was a cooking magazine. It looked boring, so Adam pushed it aside to see if there was anything more interesting to read. Underneath was a half-opened folder. Normally, he would never consider looking through someone's personal information. But what he saw made his vision blur.

There, sticking out of the folder was a newspaper article from this morning's paper. Adam's father hadn't gotten to finish reading the paper by the time Adam left. He must not have seen the article, or otherwise he surely would have shown Adam. The article featured a picture taken yesterday, a picture of Adam getting the cooler of water dumped on his head. The caption read: "Adam Hollinger was Saturday's MVP and sole pitcher as the Reds progress to the final game series."

Beneath the picture, an article followed. Adam put it aside. He could read it later. He flipped through the folder to see what else was inside, and his eyes bulged open. First, there was a list of the Autumn League roster. His named was circled, under *Lancaster Reds*. Then, there was the article that Ms. Paulus had read to the class. Again, Adam's name was circled in purple pen.

Adam thought about his *Logan Zephyr* comic. The Space Sorceress gained power by collecting personal items from Logan's crew and using the items to make potions and spells. Could Belle be doing the same thing? Patrick was never going to believe this.

"Why does she have these articles about me?" Adam whispered to Zeph.

Zeph answered with a howl.

"Fresh lemonade," Belle announced, coming down the stairs.

Adam shoved the articles back into the folder and pushed it under the cooking magazine. To avoid suspicion, he opened the magazine and pretended to be reading.

"Oh, do you like cooking?" Belle asked.

"Cooking?" Adam asked.

She pointed to the cooking magazine. Adam had opened to an article about how to make the perfect Thanksgiving feast.

Adam already felt his ears blushing.

"No," Adam said. "I was just flipping."

"Too bad," Belle said. "I love cooking. There's just something satisfying about mixing all the different ingredients to create flavors and textures in just the right proportions. It's like magic."

She placed a glass of lemonade on the table in front of Adam. Adam studied it carefully. Bits of pulp swirled around in the yellow liquid, and bits of sugar clung to the lip of the glass. Adam wondered whether it was safe to drink. He picked it up and sniffed it.

"Like it?" Belle asked.

Adam took a sip. It *tasted* like lemonade. He let the liquid linger on his tongue, trying to determine if he tasted anything magical or dangerous. He didn't taste anything strange. In fact, it was probably the best lemonade he'd ever had. But he couldn't tell Belle that.

"It's good," he said.

The two sat in silence sipping the lemonade.

"Too bad your sister's grounded."

How did Arabella know that? Adam had only just found out.

"Why is it too bad?"

"Cassie was hoping she could come over, too. Cassie wanted to talk to her. She's got a proposition to ask her."

"A proposition?"

"An offer."

Adam's mind raced with possibilities. Maybe Cassandra and Arabella were both witches. Maybe they were going to offer to turn Courtney into a witch, too. She certainly had the personality for it. Adam shuddered, imagining all the new ways Courtney could torment him if she became a witch. Being turned into a toad would be the least of his problems.

"An offer?" Adam repeated.

"Oh, just a little something Cassandra wanted to discuss with her. It wouldn't start until after Halloween."

Adam raised one brow. Why did it have to wait until Halloween? And what was *it* in the first place? With two witches going after Courtney, maybe JJ was the least of her problems. Adam remembered his father's advice about telling his parents when something was wrong. But how could he do that? His dad didn't even believe in witches. He'd never believe that two witches lived down the street, let alone that they wanted to turn Courtney into one, too.

Adam drank his lemonade more quickly. As he drank, he decided he couldn't tell his parents. Instead, he would talk to Patrick. Together, they'd figure out something.

"You look worried," Belle said.

Adam shook his head.

Belle cleared her throat. "Adam, if you know about something Courtney's doing wrong, you should tell your parents. You're a good kid, but not everyone is as good as you. Courtney seems like she needs some extra... guidance."

Adam nodded. He tried to drink his lemonade as quickly as possible without getting a stomach ache. The faster he drank, the faster he could go home.

"Wow, you're thirsty!" Without asking if he wanted more, Belle took the pitcher and refilled his glass all the way.

"Thanks," Adam said miserably.

"So, are you coming in to the comic book store anytime soon?"

"I don't know. Why?" Adam tried to sound mean. Maybe if he sounded mean, Belle would stop doing witchy things to him. What kind of neighbor kept article clippings of the kid next door?

"The next time you plan to go, you should check to see if I'm working."

"Why?"

"It'd be another chance to see my favorite neighbor," she said cheerfully.

Adam squinted. Her answer was suspicious, and he couldn't get the *Space Sorceress* out of his mind. Why did she have those articles? He reached to brush a leaf off of his shirt and felt the amulet still hanging around his neck. If Belle *was* a witch, he wanted nothing to do with it.

"Here," he said, removing the ribbon from his neck. "Thanks for the good luck. But I don't need it anymore."

"You can keep it," she said. "Keep it for your game against your next rivals—"

"The Scranton Sliders," Adam finished. "Coach just found out they won their last game, too."

Belle nodded. "And who are you playing next week after you beat the Sliders?"

"The Angels."

"The *Altoona* Angels?" she asked. "I've been researching teams in the Autumn League, and the Angels are pretty good. You should hold onto that good luck charm," she insisted.

"I'd rather win on my own skill. Not luck," Adam said.

"It's not luck," Belle said. She seemed insulted, or maybe sad. Were those tears forming in her eyes? "The amulet won't let you do anything you couldn't have done on your own. It just helps you to focus. I really want you to keep it."

Adam could tell she wouldn't take no for an answer. She took the ribbon from his hands and tied it back around his neck. "Besides," she said, "if Courtney is planning something mean to do on Halloween, maybe you should keep it at least until then."

"All right," Adam nodded.

"So what are you going to be for Halloween? Have you decided?"

"I want to be Logan Zephyr," Adam said. "He wears a green and silver space suit." Adam thought for a minute. "But I can't figure out how to make a costume like that. So I might go as a zombie pitcher instead. I could wear my old uniform—the one from my regular season. I could make my face look pale and bloody..."

"Neat," said Belle. "That was the Lancaster Lightnings, right?" she asked. "The local team you played for. They had a yellow uniform with a lightning bolt logo?"

Adam stared at her. "How did you know that?" he asked.

Belle shrugged. "I know lots of things," she said. "Especially about my favorite neighbor."

Adam's mind raced. How could she have known he played for the Lancaster Lightnings? She hadn't even been living in the neighborhood at the time. Adam glanced again at the folder of newspaper clippings. The wind blew a gust through the open window, and Adam caught a whiff of the house that smelled like, well, like Mr. Frostburg. Suddenly the room began to spin. Adam glanced around, trying to make sense of things. Was the lemonade poisoned? Why couldn't he think straight? His mind felt fuzzy, and he couldn't concentrate on remaining calm. He looked at the table where Patrick had gotten his fortune read.

"Want me to read your fortune, too?" Belle asked.

"No," Adam said quickly.

"Are you sure? I read Patrick's."

"No," Adam said again. He had to get out of her house. Maybe she was already trying to cast a spell on him. "I've got to get home," he lied. "Mom needs me, and I have a million chores to do, and I have to feed the dogs, and I think I'm supposed to clean my room, and..." He took a deep breath and chugged the rest of his lemonade. He knew he'd have a stomach ache, but anything was better than spending another minute in that house.

"Thanks for the lemonade," he said. "Come on, Zeph."

Zeph barked once and followed Adam out the back door, down the driveway, and back to the Hollinger's house. Adam walked quickly toward his house, eager to tell Patrick about the articles right away.

~ TWENTY-FOUR ~
Marnie Ellison's Secret Crush

At recess on Monday, Adam and Patrick skipped their usual dodge ball game to discuss Arabella.

"It's pretty cool," Patrick said. "Living down the street from a witch—and so close to Halloween, too."

"I don't think it's cool at all," Adam said. "Patrick, she had all kinds of newspaper clippings of me. And I'm pretty sure she put a spell on Zeph to make him fall asleep in the leaf pile. And who knows *what* was in that lemonade. Do you think I should tell my parents?"

"What can they do?" Patrick asked. "If she *is* a witch, she could put a spell on them just as easy as she could put a spell on you. Maybe they're *already* under her spell."

Adam nodded. "You might be right."

"If you think living down the street from a witch is spooky, then you don't know anything," said a voice behind Adam. It was a girl's voice, and it was coming from the monkey bars.

Adam turned around and snarled. It was Marnie Ellison. She was hanging upside-down from the monkey bars. She had been listening in on Adam and Patrick's conversation.

"Hey, you're eavesdropping," Patrick said. "Quit spying on us."

"I'm just playing on the monkey bars," she said innocently. "It's not my fault if you want to have your conversation right next to me."

"Whatever, Marnie," Patrick said. "What could possibly be scarier than living next to a witch?"

"Well," Marnie said, turning right-side-up so that she was sitting on top of the bars. "What my sister's going to do to you on Halloween, that's what."

Patrick frowned.

"What's she going to do to us on Halloween?" Adam asked.

Marnie laughed. "Not just her."

"Who else, then?" Adam asked. "And what are they going to do to us?"

"Wouldn't you like to know?" Marnie smirked.

Adam rolled his eyes, but before he could say anything, a group of girls approached.

"Hi Adam," Olivia chirped.

"Hi Olivia," Adam mumbled.

"Hi Adam," Priya said more loudly than Oliva.

"Hi Priya," Adam said quietly.

"Hi Adam," Amira squealed even more loudly than Priya.

Adam sighed. "Hi Amira," he whispered.

"Hi Adam," Melody practically shouted.

"Hi, Melody." Adam looked at Patrick. Patrick shrugged.

"We heard you won the game for your team," Olivia said. "We wanted to stop by and congratulate you."

"Thanks," Adam said. "You know, Patrick's on the team, too."

Olivia looked briefly at Patrick but turned right back to Adam.

"Congratulations, Patrick," she said, looking straight at Adam.

"You're the star pitcher," Melody said. "You should get all the credit."

"Baseball's a team sport," Adam said.

"And you're the team's star," Amira said. She stepped closer to Adam.

Adam's ears caught fire.

"I saw a picture of you in the paper," Melody said. "If I bring it in tomorrow, will you autograph it for me?"

"Me, too?" Amira added.

"And me?" asked the other girls simultaneously.

"Sure, I guess so," Adam stuttered.

"So you think you'll be at the Harvest Dance?" Melody asked.

"We're probably going to be at a baseball game," Patrick said, trying to rescue his friend.

"Yeah," Adam said. "The Autumn League championship is a three-game tournament. There's one game Friday evening, and two games on Saturday."

"It's best out of three," Patrick explained. "So if we win one game and the Angels win another, then we'll be spending Saturday afternoon playing the third game."

"But if not?" Olivia asked. "What if you don't have to play that third game?"

Marnie jumped down from the monkey bars. "Are you deaf *and* stupid?" she asked the girls. "He said he's probably going to be at a baseball game, so why don't you stop asking him, okay?"

Adam's jaw dropped.

The four girls turned their noses up at Marnie.

"Didn't you hear me?" Marnie said again. She picked up a handful of sand and threw it at the girls.

"Ouch," Melanie screamed. "She got sand in my eyes."

Amira and Olivia ran to get a teacher while Priya stayed to comfort Melanie.

"What was that all about?" Patrick asked Marnie. "Since when do you defend Adam? I thought you always gave him a hard time."

"Hmph," Marnie said. "Adam, you'd better not tell your parents about my sister and her Halloween plans. Or else."

Amira and Olivia quickly returned with Mr. Newburg, the assistant principal.

"Marnie," he said sternly, "did you throw sand at Melanie?" he asked.

"She started it," Marnie said angrily.

"Is this true?" Mr. Newburg asked.

"I didn't start anything," Melanie insisted, rubbing her eyes.

"She didn't," Olivia said. "We were just asking Adam about the Harvest Dance."

Mr. Newburg nodded. "I see. Marnie, you can't solve problems by throwing sand." He turned to Melanie. "Let's get you to the nurse. And Marnie, you'll have to come to my office. I'm afraid you'll have to have detention." Mr. Newburg gave Adam a stern glare, as if this was partly his fault. Then he turned back toward the school.

Marnie glared at Olivia, Priya, and Amira as she followed Mr. Newburg and Melanie into the school.

When they were out of sight, Olivia, Priya, and Amira hurried to the other side of dodge ball court without even saying good-bye. When she saw no one was looking, Olivia pulled out her cell phone and started to text something.

"Girls," Patrick said. "Who can ever understand them?"

Adam shrugged in agreement.

~ * ~

That afternoon, Coach Harris scheduled practice at Stoney Brook Elementary School. It wasn't the field they normally used, but it was the only one available. Adam and Patrick got special permission to stay at school until practice started.

They stayed with Mr. Macintyre, the gym teacher, until their coach arrived.

"Adam," Mr. Macintyre said, "I saw a group of girls bugging you at recess. And I heard someone was throwing sand. Everything all right?"

"Yes," Adam sighed.

"They all want to go to the Harvest Dance with him," Patrick explained. "And Adam doesn't like any of them."

"They only like me now because I'm a pitcher for the Lancaster Reds. Before that, they didn't even know I existed. Besides, I don't want to go to the dance with *anyone*."

Mr. Macintyre laughed. "Girls," he said. "They start driving you crazy in fifth grade, and they never let up." He smiled. "Until you find the right one."

"I don't think any of them are as crazy as Marnie Ellison," Patrick said.

"Marnie, eh?" Mr. Macintyre asked. "Is she the one who threw sand?"

"Yeah," Adam said. "She's the sister of my sister's best friend. They talk about me all the time. She torments me. She brushes eraser dust on me. She trips me. And she spreads rumors about me."

"You know what they say about girls who tease you, don't you?" Mr. Macintyre asked with a twinkle in his eye.

"No," Adam said. "What do they say?"

"They say girls only tease you if they have a crush on you," he explained.

"Eww, gross. So it's true, then," Patrick said. "Marnie Ellison has a crush on Adam. Maybe that's why she threw sand at those other girls today. She was jealous of them because they were talking to you, and trying to get you to go to the dance with them."

"Quiet," Adam whispered. His ears were burning again.

Luckily, Coach Harris showed up just in time to change the conversation. Adam could never have been more relieved for practice to begin.

~ TWENTY-FIVE ~
The Table Turns

After practice, Adam was tired and hungry. It was already getting dark out, so he was surprised when Courtney showed up on foot. He had been expecting his mother to come with her minivan.

"Nice job at practice, dork," she said. She was wearing JJ's blue jean jacket.

"Yeah, dork," a deep voice said from the shadows. JJ stepped into the light and started laughing. He wore a black leather jacket, and his hair was more spiky than usual. Meghan and Aileen stepped out from behind him.

"Why are you here?" Adam asked.

Courtney laughed. "You should know."

Adam didn't understand. "What do you mean?"

"You should know why we're here. You're the one that got Marnie in trouble."

"Me? I didn't do anything."

"She's been texting us all afternoon from detention, saying it's *your* fault she's there. She was trying to defend you from some girls who were bugging you."

"I never asked her to do that," Adam said. His ears started turning red. "Besides, if she has detention, how can she be texting you?"

Aileen laughed as her cell phone beeped. "The detention teacher's so stupid. He's reading the newspaper instead of watching her. She's been texting me all afternoon, and the teacher has no clue."

Adam shook his head.

"Listen," Aileen said. "If you hurt my sister, I'll have JJ beat you up."

Courtney, Aileen, and Meghan laughed.

"And I'm pretty good at beating people up," JJ said in a gruff voice.

"Why would I hurt Marnie? I'd never punch a girl."

"She's not talking about punching, you idiot," Courtney said. "She means if you ever hurt Marnie's feelings..."

"Her feelings?" Adam asked. "What do you mean?"

"If you're too stupid to know, then I'm not going to be the one to tell you," Courtney said.

"Yeah, Adam," Aileen agreed. "Get a clue, already."

Adam shook his head. "So Mom's not coming?"

"Wow, your brother really *is* stupid," Meghan said.

Courtney explained. "Mom said we could all walk to the elementary school to pick up Marnie after detention. She said while we were here, we should tell you to walk home with us."

Adam groaned. The last thing he felt like doing was walking home. He lived less than a mile from the school, but he had his school bag and his favorite bat and his baseball mitt. His body was already sore from practicing so much, and from raking the leaves in Belle's yard.

"Adam, you need a ride home?" Coach Harris asked. He eyed the group of kids suspiciously. "You kids okay here?"

Adam started to answer, but Courtney shoved him to the side and answered for him. "Our mom wants him to walk home with us. She's busy making lasagna," she said sweetly.

Adam's mouth watered.

"Okay, then," Coach Harris said. "Walk safely. You'll all be safe in such a big group. Just go straight home, okay? And Courtney, you have a cell phone in case anything happens?"

She held up her sparkling phone. "Of course."

"Bye, Adam," Patrick called.

Adam waved, wishing he could have gotten a ride with Patrick.

As Coach Harris drove away, Mr. Gutten, the detention teacher, came out of the school. Marnie and three other sullen-looking students followed. The three students filed quietly into their parents' waiting cars.

"Is one of you Aileen Ellison?" Mr. Gutten asked.

"I am," Aileen said.

"Your mother telephoned the school. Marnie is supposed to walk home with you."

"I know," Aileen said angrily. "I'm not stupid. Why else would I even be here?"

Mr. Gutten shook his head. "You kids be careful walking home. It's getting dark."

"I know that too," Aileen said. "We're not stupid babies. We're in seventh grade, so we know what we're doing."

Mr. Gutten looked at JJ suspiciously. "And he's in seventh grade too?"

"Maybe not," Courtney grabbed JJ's hand, giggled, and skipped away.

"He's my older brother," Meghan explained. "He's making sure we get home safely."

Mr. Gutten nodded.

Marnie sullenly joined the group.

"Way to go," Aileen told her sister once Mr. Gutten was out of earshot. "Your first detention. You should be proud."

"No, you shouldn't," Adam said. "Those girls weren't doing anything to you. You didn't have to throw sand at them."

"They were bothering me," Marnie said.

Adam shook his head. The group—Courtney, Aileen, Meghan, JJ, and Marnie—had already started walking home. Adam scrambled to grab his school bag and baseball gear. Even though they weren't his favorite group of people, he preferred their company to walking alone.

They walked by the spooky old house on the corner of Brookside Drive and Elementary Alley. A chill shot down Adam's spine. He quickened his pace, but he kept himself about twenty feet behind the others.

In the twilight, he could see Courtney whisper something in JJ's ear. JJ giggled, then cleared his throat.

"You want to know what I heard?" he asked loudly.

"What did you hear?" Courtney said, just as loudly. It was clear they were speaking for Adam's benefit.

Adam cringed.

"I heard," JJ continued, "that your little slime ball of a brother is thinking about telling your parents that we have Halloween plans."

"I heard that too," Courtney said.

"Oh no," Meghan said, a little too over-dramatically. "What *ever* will you do about it?"

"Well," JJ said, "there's really only one thing we can do."

With that, the group stopped. Adam slowed his pace, but they waited for him anyway. JJ grabbed Adam by the collar of his shirt and shook him. Adam was strong, but JJ was twice his size.

Adam froze.

"If you ruin our Halloween plans, you little twerp," JJ threatened, "then this is just a taste of what you'll get. Got it?"

Adam tried to speak, but nothing would come out. He nodded instead. He already felt sweat dripping down his back.

"Do you think he gets it?" JJ asked.

"Shake him once more," Courtney demanded.

JJ did as she asked, then pushed Adam to the ground.

The group laughed and started walking again. Adam saw Courtney put her arm around JJ's waist. JJ didn't seem to react.

Marnie stayed at the back of the group. When the group had moved out of earshot, she crept over to Adam, who was still sitting on the ground.

"JJ's kind of a jerk," Marnie said.

"Marnie," Adam said. "I didn't make you get detention. Why is everyone saying I did?"

Marnie stuttered.

"I didn't give you detention, Marnie."

"Adam?" Marnie asked. "Do you like Olivia?"

Adam was glad it was getting dark. He didn't have to worry about his ears turning red.

"No," he said.

"Do you like Melanie?"

"No," he answered.

"Priya?"

"No."

"Amira?"

"No."

Marnie paused. "Do you like anyone?"

"Marnie," Aileen called. "Stay with us."

"Coming," Marnie called to the group. She turned back to Adam and gave him a hand to help him up.

"Thanks," he said.

"I could carry your glove," she said. "I mean since you have your bat and your schoolbag, too."

"Okay," Adam said. Marnie bent down to pick up Adam's baseball glove. Adam couldn't tell for sure in the darkness, but Marnie seemed to smile.

"If you don't like any of those girls," Marnie said, "then you should tell them you're not going to the Harvest Dance with them."

"I don't want to hurt their feelings," Adam said.

"It would be better if you just told them no, rather than dragging it out."

Adam grunted. "Like I said, I don't want to hurt their feelings."

"Then we need to find another way for you to tell them you can't go with them."

"I tried. I'm out of ideas," Adam said. "And so is Patrick." Adam wondered why Marnie wanted to help him. She was usually busy making fun of him.

Quietly, Adam and Marnie fell into step about thirty feet behind the others. All they heard were the sounds of an occasional owl hooting or a car driving by.

"I guess I have one more idea you could try," Marnie said finally.

"What idea is that?" Adam asked. He shifted his schoolbag.

"Well..."

"Well what?"

"I guess you could go to the Harvest Dance with *me*."

"With you?"

"Sure," Marnie said. "That way, those girls would stop bugging you."

"I guess it *would* get them to stop bugging me. But why would you want to go to the Harvest Dance with me? I thought you hated me. You're always tormenting me at school and at home." Adam thought about it for a minute. "I'll bet you're just doing this as a part of Courtney or Aileen's plan. You're going to go to the dance with me just so you can plan some new way to humiliate me in front of the whole school."

"That's not true," Marnie said.

"Would you tell me if it *was* true?"

By the light of the passing headlights, Adam could see that Marnie had her hands on her hips and was staring at him with her mouth open. "Adam Hollinger, I could just—"

But before she could explain what she could just do, a car pulled up to the curb near Courtney and the others. It was Mrs. Ellison. "I got out of my meeting early," she said. "Get in. It's getting dark."

Marnie took Adam's baseball glove and threw it at him as hard as she could. It took Adam by surprise, so he paused as Marnie sprinted to her mother's car.

"Is Adam with you?" he heard Mrs. Ellison ask.

"No," Marnie lied. "He got a ride home with Patrick."

Adam watched in amazement as the car drove away, and he was forced to walk the final leg of the journey home by himself—in the dark.

~ * ~

When he finally made it home, Courtney, Meghan, and JJ were in the driveway waiting for him. Courtney was no longer wearing JJ's blue jean jacket, and she shivered in the cold.

"Give me your bag," Courtney ordered.

"No," Adam said and tried to push past them.

"JJ," Courtney said, "take care of him."

JJ laughed and grabbed Adam from behind. JJ held Adam's arms while Courtney took Adam's bag and Meghan took Adam's baseball bat.

"Now," Courtney said, while Adam was held against his will. "When we get inside, you tell Mom that we all walked back together. You tell her you had a nice time at practice. If you mention anything about walking home by yourself, or about our plans for Halloween, you're dead meat."

Adam swallowed hard. "But I don't even know what your plans *are* for Halloween."

Courtney and Meghan giggled. "Good," Courtney said. "Let's keep it that way."

Courtney led the way inside, followed by Meghan. JJ finally let Adam go and disappeared into the shadows.

Courtney and Meghan headed right for the kitchen. There, Mrs. Hollinger was at the stove making garlic bread. The whole place smelled like lasagna. Courtney waited until her mom turned around before plopping Adam's bag onto the floor.

"Hi girls," Mrs. Hollinger said. "Did you have a nice walk back?"

Courtney shrugged. "It was okay," she said. "But Adam's bag sure is heavy. We offered to carry it for him. Now my arm is so tired."

"That was nice of you, Courtney," Mrs. Hollinger said as Adam entered the kitchen. "Adam, since Courtney and Meghan carried your bags for you, why don't you set the table tonight? I know it's Courtney's turn, but she looks so tired."

Adam opened his mouth to protest, but Courtney gave him a mean look, and he reluctantly closed his mouth, washed his hands, and set the table for dinner.

~ TWENTY-SIX ~
Scary, Shiny, and Spells

On Friday night, Mr. and Mrs. Hollinger had an announcement to make. They decided to allow Courtney to stay home alone during Adam's game against the Scranton Sliders.

Adam crossed his arms and pouted. Courtney never *really* got into trouble.

"She seems like she's making an effort to change since we had our little talk," Mrs. Hollinger explained to Adam. "She carried your books home earlier this week when you two walked home from practice."

Adam rolled his eyes. She had done nothing of the sort.

"Are you at least keeping her cell phone?" Adam asked.

"We'll let her keep her cell phone while we're gone," Mr. Hollinger said. "In case of an emergency."

"But if she's home, won't the home phone be available for emergencies?" Adam asked, crossing his arms.

Mrs. Hollinger wavered. "I had thought of that," she said. "But Courtney might need her phone while she's out walking the dogs."

"You're going to trust her alone with the dogs?" Adam asked. He wondered whether he'd ever see Zeph again. Why were Mom and Dad always so lenient with Courtney?

"I don't see why she gets to stay," Adam said.

"We have to give her a chance," Mrs. Hollinger said. "We thought it would be a nice gesture that might build trust between us and Courtney. If she does well, we can trust her again. And by letting her stay home, we're showing her that we trust her."

"You shouldn't trust her," Adam mumbled.

"Besides," Mr. Hollinger explained, "the field where you'll be playing the Sliders doesn't allow dogs. Someone's gotta stay home to watch the puppies."

"Got *to*," Mrs. Hollinger whispered.

Adam looked down at Zeph.

"I don't know if that's such a good idea. Are you really going to trust Courtney with the dogs, let alone with herself?"

"Don't worry," Mrs. Hollinger added. "We're going to ask Belle to keep an eye on the place—and on Courtney—while we're gone. Belle told us that she and Cassandra might stop by once or twice to check on Courtney."

That was all Adam needed to hear. He didn't know which was worse—leaving the corgis with Courtney, or asking Belle to keep an eye on things. The last time Courtney was trusted to watch the puppies, Sapphie escaped, and Adam still couldn't figure out how she got loose. He couldn't imagine coming home from his game to find Zeph missing, too. And what if Belle and Cassandra were still thinking about turning Courtney into a witch?

Adam's parents went downstairs, and Adam sat on the kitchen floor to pet Zeph. The more he thought about it, the clearer the solution became. And the clearer the solution became, the less he liked it.

"I can't believe what I'm about to do," Adam said to Zeph, "but we're going to take a trip to

Belle's house."

~ * ~

Cassandra answered the door. "Adam," she said cheerfully. "Zeph."

She was wearing her cape and a long, dark dress underneath. She had painted her nails a dark, hideous green that almost looked black.

"Hi Cassandra," Adam said grumpily. "Is Belle at home?"

"Sure is," Cassandra said. "She's going to be so happy to see you."

Adam didn't respond. Instead, he stared at Cassandra's strange outfit.

"Oh, you'll have to excuse my appearance," she said. "I've got a very special appointment." She cleared her throat and waved her hands in the air as she chanted: "Round about the cauldron go, in the poison'd entrails throw... Toad, that under cold stone days and nights has thirty-one sweltere'd venom sleeping got. Boil thou first i'the charmed pot." She giggled. "Wish me luck."

Adam took two steps back as Cassandra dashed past him, hurried to the driveway, got into her car, and drove down the street.

"Did you hear that?" Adam asked Zeph. His ears prickled. "If I ever heard a witch's spell, that was it. I don't want to be turned into a toad, do you?"

Zeph howled in response.

Belle pranced down the stairs. "Did I hear my favorite neighbor?" she asked.

"Hi Belle," Adam mumbled without making eye contact.

"Hi, neighbor," Belle said, giving him a friend-ly punch in the arm. "And Zeph," she said, patting the pup on the head.

Immediately, Zeph tumbled to the floor and rolled onto his back, allowing Belle to rub his belly.

"I sort of need your help," Adam said, want-ing to get the conversation over as quickly as possi-ble.

"Anything," Belle offered.

"My parents are letting my stupid sister stay home alone with the dogs tomorrow."

"I know," Belle said. "Tomorrow's the day of your big game."

"Yeah, against the Sliders."

"So how can I help?"

"It's not that I care so much about Courtney," Adam said, "but I don't trust her to watch Zeph. Or Sapphie, for that matter. I was wondering if you could..."

"Keep an eye on things?" she asked.

"Yes," Adam said. "I know my parents asked you to already. They trust Courtney a lot more than they should. Can you make sure Zeph stays safe while we're gone? I mean, every time Courtney's supposed to watch the dogs, something bad happens. They chew something dangerous, they get loose, or whatever."

"I'll be glad to," Arabella said, patting Zeph again.

"Thanks," Adam mumbled. He turned to leave and hoped Belle didn't offer him cider or lemonade or potion.

"Oh, Adam, one thing before you leave."

Adam cringed and turned back to face Belle.

"I've got something special for you," she said.

"What's that?" Adam asked.

She ran to the living room and returned with a clear plastic box. "You mentioned you wanted to go as Logan Zephyr for Halloween. I just couldn't help it."

Adam's jaw dropped as he looked at the box. It was a perfect replica of Logan Zephyr's uniform: a dark green suit with shiny silver boots.

"How did you get that?" Adam asked.

"Let's just say it was a little Halloween magic," Belle said.

"Halloween magic," Adam repeated. Was Belle admitting to being a sorceress? Maybe asking her to keep an eye on Courtney wasn't such a good idea.

Belle handed him the box. "I was going to wait to give this to you, but I just can't resist."

"Wow," Adam said. He looked up at Belle. "Thanks." Adam knelt down to show Zeph the outfit. "This is the uniform of the guy you were named after," Adam explained.

Zeph took one look at the shiny silver boots and howled. He tugged and tugged on his leash and hid behind Belle.

"What's wrong?" Adam asked.

But Zeph wouldn't come out until Adam had closed the box.

"What's wrong with this costume?" Adam asked.

"Nothing," Belle said. "I don't know why Zeph's acting that way."

Belle petted Zeph, which seemed to comfort him.

Adam knelt down, costume box in hand, and called to Zeph.

Zeph wouldn't come.

"Did you cast a spell on my dog?" Adam asked.

"What? A spell?"

"Just forget about tomorrow," Adam said. "I'm sure Courtney will be fine by herself."

Adam placed the costume box on the floor.

"We're going home, Zeph," he insisted.

Zeph followed, careful to avoid the costume box.

"But Adam, I..." Belle said as Adam hurried out the door.

Because he didn't look back, he didn't see the sad expression on Belle's face as he disappeared down the drive without his Logan Zephyr costume.

~ TWENTY-SEVEN ~
Two Callers

"It's so quiet. Where's Adam?" Sapphie asked from her crate.

"At his baseball game," Zeph said. "Don't you listen to anything?"

"Where's Mom and Dad?" Sapphie asked.

"At the game, Sapphie," Zeph answered.

"My Courtney, too?" Sapphie asked.

Zeph growled. "Don't you listen to anything? Adam explained this all before he left. Courtney's upstairs sleeping. When she wakes up, she's going to let us out of our little houses and take us outside to play. Adam promised."

"They should have taken us to the game," Sapphie said. "Remember the last game? All that food that we ate under the bleachers."

"Don't you remember the trouble you got into?" Zeph asked.

"I love getting into trouble," Sapphie admitted.

"I don't like it at all," Zeph said. "I like when Adam tells me I'm being good."

"Hmph," Sapphie said. "You're sooo boring. You won't like today, then. We're going to get into lots of trouble."

"What do you mean?" Zeph asked.

Before Sapphie could answer, the doorbell rang. Sapphie and Zeph erupted in a round of barking. They loved when the doorbell rang. It meant more people were here.

A minute later, Courtney trudged down the stairs, still in her pajamas.

"Coming," Courtney muttered.

"Who do you think is there?" Zeph asked.

"I don't know," Sapphie said.

"JJ," Courtney said at the front door. "I wasn't expecting you here so soon. Come on in. I have to get dressed."

A moment later, JJ and Courtney appeared at the kitchen entryway. Sapphie went hysterical, barking and clawing at her crate.

Zeph stayed quiet, but the fur on the back of his neck stood straight up.

"Want to play with the dogs?" Courtney asked.

"No," JJ said. "Leave them in their cages. I'm hungry."

"I can make you something to eat," Courtney said. "Grilled cheese? Soup? Oatmeal?"

"Oatmeal?" JJ asked. "How lame. I'll take two grilled cheese sandwiches. No, make that three."

"Okay," Courtney said.

JJ stuck his tongue out at Sapphie as he exited the kitchen. Sapphie stopped barking long enough to hear him trudge down the stairs and turn on the television.

"I don't like this one bit," Zeph said after Courtney went downstairs with JJ's three grilled cheese sandwiches. "I heard Courtney's parents tell her that she wasn't allowed to have guests over."

"Oh Zeph, you're no fun," Sapphie said. Sapphie barked and barked until Courtney finally came back to the kitchen.

"You dogs be quiet," Courtney said. "I'm trying to impress JJ. We need to make Halloween plans, and I don't need you dogs distracting us."

Sapphie quieted and tried to look as cute as possible.

"Oh, all right," Courtney said finally. "You can come with me—if you promise to be good."

Sapphie sat quietly as Courtney opened the cage.

Courtney narrowed her eyes. "Zeph can stay in his crate, though," she said spitefully. "I'm done doing favors for Adam."

~ * ~

Zeph sat alone in the kitchen for hours. He strained his huge ears to try to hear what was happening downstairs. All he could hear was the hum of the television and an occasional bark from Sapphie. Every now and then, JJ laughed menacingly. Zeph knew JJ wasn't supposed to be in the house, but he couldn't do a thing about it. Even if he escaped from the crate, what could he do against such a scary person?

At one point, Courtney came into the kitchen to answer the phone. Zeph listened to Courtney's side of the conversation and tried to figure out what was going on. A moment later, JJ came into the kitchen carrying Sapphie. Sapphie glanced happily at her brother. She loved being carried around. After Courtney hung up the phone, she turned to JJ.

"That was my parents," she said. "Apparently Adam was the starting pitcher today. He almost pitched a shut-out. The other team got very few hits and only two runs in the second game. Both games ended faster than expected, and they're on their way home."

"When will they be back?" he asked.

"They're over an hour away," Courtney said, "so we still have time. Maybe we can watch another movie," she suggested.

"Eh," JJ said. "That's kind of boring."

"Oh," Courtney said.

Zeph barked.

"Quiet, Zeph," Courtney said.

"Maybe we could play some of your brother's video games," JJ said.

Zeph plopped down in his crate, hoping Adam would be home soon. Just when Zeph was out of ideas, the doorbell rang again.

"Did you invite anyone over?" Courtney called asked JJ.

"No," JJ said.

"I don't know who it could be, then," Courtney said. "It can't be my parents already. They'd ground me for life if they caught you here."

Courtney peeked out the kitchen window. "It's Belle. Quick, JJ. You've got to get out of here. She'll tell my parents you were here for sure."

"Geez, Courtney," JJ said. "It's such a pain always having to sneak around. Maybe I have better things to do than play hide-and-seek from your neighbors."

"What can I do about it, JJ?" Courtney asked.

"Whatever. I'm out of here," JJ mumbled. He put Sapphie down and disappeared down the stairs. Courtney followed. The back door opened, and then slammed shut.

A moment later, the front door opened.

"Hi, Belle," Courtney said.

"Hi, Courtney," Belle said. "I brought over a pizza. I thought you could use some company—and some food."

"Wow. Thanks," Courtney said.

"I'm not interrupting anything, am I?" Belle asked.

"No, of course not."

"I thought you'd be lonely," Belle said strangely. "You know, being here *all by yourself* for so long."

"Yeah," Courtney lied. "All by myself..."

By now, Sapphie had joined Courtney and was barking at the front door.

"Hi, Sapphie," Belle said. "Where's your brother? Where's Zeph?"

"Um, he's in the kitchen," Courtney said.

"Why is he up there by himself?"

Zeph couldn't help but bark as Belle's footsteps grew louder and louder on the front steps. By the time Belle came into the kitchen, Zeph was howling with delight. He was so happy to be let out of his crate that he didn't even notice the boxed Halloween costume Belle left on the kitchen table— even with its scary foil accents.

~ TWENTY-EIGHT ~
Foil Boots and Goblin's Tooth

Halloween was on a Thursday this year, which meant trick-or-treating had to wrap up early. As parents loved to remind their children, "it *is* a school night..." Still, none of the teachers gave homework, and Coach Harris gave the boys the day off from practice. The following day, Friday, was the first big game against the Altoona Angels, and the boys needed all the rest they could get.

After a quiet week at school, Courtney was spending the evening at Meghan's house with Aileen. Adam and Patrick decided to trick-or-treat in Adam's neighborhood, since there were more houses—and that meant more candy.

The two of them got ready in Adam's room. Zeph and Sapphie sat on the floor watching them with a mixture of fear and interest.

"You really think I should wear this Logan Zephyr outfit?" Adam asked.

He looked at the space uniform, newly-pressed in the box. The green suit looked exactly like the one from the comics, and Adam had never seen cooler-looking space boots than the foil ones that came with the uniform.

"I don't know," Patrick said. "Do you think she put a spell on it?"

Adam shrugged. "She left it here last Saturday. She came to check on Courtney while we were at the game. It had a note taped to the box that said *Thank-you for raking*." Adam studied the uniform. "It sure looks cool," he admitted. He turned to the puppies. "You guys think I should wear this?"

Sapphie got so excited that she jumped up on Adam's bed, wrestling with his pillow.

"What about you, Zeph?" Adam asked.

Zeph sat at attention, trying to figure out what Adam was asking.

Adam held out the green uniform, allowing Zeph to sniff it.

Zeph sniffed and sniffed. Finally, he let out an approving howl and wagged his tail.

"I guess Zeph's okay with it," Adam said. Hesitantly, he stepped into the uniform. Looking in the mirror, even he had to admit it was the coolest Halloween costume he'd ever worn.

"Now for the boots," Adam said.

He took the foil boots from the package. They crinkled as he held them.

Zeph took one look at the foil and squealed. Sapphie let out a happy yelp as she watched her brother dash under the bed.

"Wow," Patrick said. "I've never seen your dog act like that."

"You think there's something wrong with the boots?" Adam asked.

"It sure seems like it," said Patrick. "Maybe they're cursed."

"I don't know," Adam said. "Are you sure a witch could really do something like that? Are you sure witches even exist? My dad thinks—"

"How else could you explain the red charm? It helped you win against two teams so far. I mean, you almost pitched a shut-out last time. How could you do that without magic?"

"You're right about that. Zeph, come out here," Adam commanded.

Slowly, Zeph crept out from under the bed. Sapphie, on top of the bed, jumped down and grabbed one of his ears. She pulled happily.

"Zeph," Adam asked, "what's wrong with my boots?"

Zeph took one look at the foil, howled again, and backed up under the bed.

Adam put on the boots and studied himself in the mirror. "Zeph'll never come trick-or-treating if I wear these boots," Adam complained. "But these are the coolest boots I've ever seen."

"We can leave Zeph here," Patrick suggested. "Even I have to admit that your costume is pretty cool."

"Okay," Adam sighed. "I'll go as Logan Zephyr. Sorry, Zeph," he said to the puppy under the bed. "You'll have a better night if you stay here. That way you won't be scared of anything."

"For a dog, he is kind of a scaredy-cat," Patrick admitted.

Adam reached under the bed to pet Zeph. "He means well, though. He's a good boy."

In the meantime, Patrick spread a glob of green on his face. "I'll be the grossest goblin ever," he said.

Sapphie took one look, yelped, and ran out of the room. She took refuge in Mr. and Mrs. Hollinger's bedroom.

"Are they boys scaring you, honey?" Mrs. Hollinger asked the frightened pup as she folded some towels.

While Adam's back was turned, Zeph followed his sister. He dashed behind Mr. Hollinger's night table, trembling every time he heard those shiny boots crinkle.

"It's going to be a long night for those dogs," Mr. Hollinger said, grabbing a stack of folded laundry to put in the linen closet. "Maybe we'd best put them in the backyard. That way they won't go crazy every time the doorbell rings, and they won't be scared by all the kids in costume."

"That's a good idea," Mrs. Hollinger said.

"Adam," she called. "Will you let the dogs out back?"

"Zeph," Adam called. "Sapphie." The corgis peeked into the hallway, took one look at Adam's shiny boots and Patrick's creepy face, and dashed under Mr. and Mrs. Hollinger's bed.

"Never mind," Mrs. Hollinger said. "I'll take them out later."

Adam nodded and closed his door so that his parents couldn't hear what he was about to say.

"Do you have any idea what my stupid sister is planning tonight?" Adam asked. "Have you heard any rumors?"

"Someone at school told me that she and JJ are going to scare kids who are trick-or-treating. That's all I heard."

"They won't be able to scare anyone. Nothing could be scarier than living down the hall from Courtney," Adam joked. "Besides, we're expecting it, right? They can't scare us if we know what's coming."

Patrick laughed. "Yeah," he agreed. "JJ's full of hot air anyway."

Adam put the finishing touches on his costume by drawing a star-shaped birthmark under his left ear.

"You look great," Patrick said.

Patrick put a brown vest over his black shirt. "Do I look like a goblin?"

"Not really," Adam said. "You still look too nice. And too human."

"Oh," Patrick said. "I almost forgot." He reached into his bag and pulled out some hideous false teeth. They were yellow and misshapen. He stuck them in his mouth and smiled at Adam.

"*Now* you look like a goblin," Adam said.

Both boys laughed.

"Hey," Patrick asked seriously, taking out his goblin teeth. "Do you think we have any chance of winning against the Angels?"

Adam shook his head. "Not from what I heard. We all know that each boy on the team has his own private coach, and they all take private lessons all year round."

"Hmm," Patrick said. "Who has time for that?"

"We'll just play our best. It's the best two out of three games."

Patrick laughed. "You'd better play your best, Adam," Patrick said. "Or else you'll have to go to the Harvest Dance. Who are you going with, Olivia?"

Adam's ears turned red. "I didn't tell you this, but I promised Marnie I'd go with her." Adam sighed heavily.

Patrick seemed to jump out of his skin. "What?"

"She was acting so weird. First, she offered to go with me. I agreed because it would be a way of avoiding those other girls. But I didn't understand why Marnie would help me out like that. Based on how she's been tormenting me for the past year, you'd think she'd *want* to see me tortured by those other girls. When I asked her why she was willing to help me out, she wouldn't answer me. She got mad and stormed off. I'll never understand girls."

"I don't want to tell you what I think," Patrick said.

"Why not?" Adam asked. "What do you think?"

"I think she's acting that way because she has a crush on you," Patrick said, and tried not to laugh.

"That's not the first time I've heard that."

"Well, going to the dance with her won't be so bad. Maybe if you do, she'll stop acting crazy every time she sees you."

Adam rolled his eyes. "Girls," he said. "They make the world so complicated."

Adam looked out his window. Across the street, he could see Belle and Cassandra's house. Belle was on her front porch changing the porch lighting from a regular light bulb to an orange one.

"Speaking of girls," Adam said. "Let's stay away from Belle's house."

"I agree," Patrick said. "I'm still creeped out by Cassandra's fortune. Beware of something like a bird—like wings. That sounds like our game against the Angels. But something big and white?"

"And a masquerade ball?" Adam asked. "Maybe it's just nonsense."

"I don't know," Patrick said. "Belle and Cassandra seem so weird. You saw how Zeph reacted to the Halloween costume Belle gave you. If they *are* witches, then the last place we want to be on Halloween is their house."

"Agreed," Adam said.

"Boys," Mrs. Hollinger called. "You can open your door now. The dogs are out in the back yard.

Besides, I want to get a picture of you before you go."

~ * ~

Outside, the neighborhood was more deserted than usual. The moon was nearly full, and fog hung in the air. A neighbor was playing a Halloween horror soundtrack from the second-story window, so every now and then a witch would cackle, a crow would caw, and a werewolf would howl.

"Creepy," Patrick said.

"Yeah," Adam agreed.

They went from house to house, careful to avoid Belle's house at the top of the hill. Since the street was so deserted, everyone gave them lots of candy. The Davenports even gave out whole candy bars, rather than the mini size.

When they had gone to all the houses on the block, Adam glanced at his watch. "We still have thirty minutes," he said. "Want to hit one more street?"

Just then, a white minivan's tires screeched as it skidded to a halt at the stop sign. Adam and Patrick jumped onto the grass to avoid getting their toes run over. The tires screeched once more as it accelerated, then slowed down as it passed Adam and Patrick as close to the grass as possible.

"Take it easy," Adam said under his breath, more to himself than to anyone else.

"Did you recognize that car?" Patrick asked.

"No. Did you?"

"No."

"They should be more careful with trick-or-treaters around," Adam said, and put a hand on his chest. "That kinda freaked me out. Maybe we should head back."

Patrick shook his head. "Let's go to all the houses on this street. I won't go home until this bag is full of candy."

"All right," Adam agreed, and he followed Patrick into the darkness.

~ TWENTY-NINE ~
The Big White Fright

In the backyard, Sapphie stayed behind the compost pile perfecting the shape of her escape tunnel.

"What are you doing, Sapphie?" Zeph asked.

"Have you noticed I'm growing every day? I need to keep expanding my adventure tunnel. That way I can escape—I mean, go on adventures, whenever I choose."

"You're going to get in trouble for getting dirty," Zeph warned. "And you know what that means. A ba..." Zeph couldn't bring himself to say the name of the terrible, wet, soapy punishment for digging in the back yard.

"Even that couldn't be scarier than what we saw earlier tonight," Sapphie said. "Could you believe what happened to Patrick? He turned into a monster!"

"I know," Zeph agreed. "And Adam had those horrible boots on. The way they looked in the light was terrible. And the crinkling noise they made, that was the worst."

Sapphie laughed. "They're just foil, Zeph," she said. "Even I know that. And *you're* supposed to be the smart one."

Zeph plopped down on the ground. No matter what Sapphie said, foil was scary.

"I'm bored, Zeph," Sapphie said when she was finished digging. "When are Courtney and Adam coming back?"

"I don't know," Zeph said. "I feel like we've been out here forever. I wonder what Adam's doing."

"I don't know," Sapphie said. "But I sure know what Courtney's doing. I can't wait to hear all about it. In fact, I want to know now, now, *now!*"

Zeph growled. "You still haven't told me what she's up to," he warned. "Is she still planning on scaring Adam?"

Sapphie took a running leap onto Zeph and bit his ear. "That's for me to know and you to find out," she howled.

With that, she dashed through the hole and appeared on the other side of the fence, wagging her little tail.

"Where are you going?" Zeph asked.

"I want to visit my friend, Belle," Sapphie said. "She always gives me fun stuff to chew on. What color scarf do you think she'll give me tonight?"

"You're not supposed to visit Belle," Zeph reminded her. "You're supposed to stay here. Didn't you hear our People tell us to stay?" Zeph barked and barked, but nothing could convince Sapphie to come back.

"Oh Zeph," Sapphie said. "When will you learn? Following the rules just isn't any fun!"

~ * ~

By the time Adam and Patrick were due home their bags of candy were so heavy, the circulation in their hands was cut off.

"I'm going to be eating candy until Valentine's Day," Adam said.

"I'll finish mine a lot faster than that," Patrick said.

Adam nodded. "We'd better hurry. Your dad should be at my house to pick you up any minute."

The boys hurried down the street. They shuffled under the weight of their candy. "I wish we'd get back already. This green goblin makeup's starting to itch."

They trudged through the crisp leaves along the side of the road. Soon, they were standing back at Adam's house, in front of the driveway.

"My dad's car isn't here yet," Patrick said. "What do you say we take one last walk to the other end of your street? You know, past Belle and Cassandra's house."

Adam's eyes grew wide. "Why?"

"Wouldn't it be cool to see real witches on Halloween?" Just as Patrick spoke, hideous cackling from the neighbor's soundtrack echoed through the air, followed by a howling werewolf.

"I don't know," Adam said. "Ever since I found those newspaper clippings of me, I've tried to steer clear."

"Hmm," Patrick said. "I think if we stayed in the street, they wouldn't be able to put any spells on us. Besides, your boots haven't done anything bad yet."

Adam shrugged. "I guess you're right."

The two boys flung their bags of candy over their shoulders and continued down the street.

The moon slipped behind a cloud, and all of a sudden, the spooky Halloween sound effects went quiet.

"I guess the neighbors are going to bed," Adam whispered. The neighborhood was quiet. Too quiet. It had been less scary with the spooky sound effects.

Patrick agreed. "It's dark at this end of the street. Maybe we should go back." The boys looked up at the moon, which still illuminated the misty fog.

Before Adam could agree, a pair of headlights sped up the road. It was the same white minivan that had driven close to them earlier, and now it was swerving from one side of the road to the next. Adam and Patrick jumped up on the Stoys' lawn to get out of the way.

Then the minivan screeched to a halt just in front of Adam and Patrick. The window rolled down, and a man in a red ski-mask shouted at them.

"Get in!" His voice was gruff and harsh.

The door to the minivan opened, and the man stuck his gloved hand out the window. He pointed fiercely to the door.

"I said to *get in*."

Adam and Patrick dropped their bags of candy and ran halfway up the Stoys' lawn. "Go ring their doorbell," Patrick shouted to Adam.

"The Stoys go to bed early," Adam yelled back. "They hate kids and Halloween and don't answer their door for Trick-or-Treaters." It was true—their porch light wasn't even on.

Slowly, the minivan drove closer to the boys, as close to the lawn as it could get.

"Get in, boys."

"What'll we do?" Patrick screamed to Adam.

"Run to Belle's house!"

Adam and Patrick put all their fears of Arabella and Cassandra aside as they ran as fast as they could toward the porch with the strange orange light.

~ THIRTY ~
Confronting the Witches

On Belle and Cassandra's porch, the creepy orange light threw strange shadows on the side of the house. The cobwebs she'd put up and the plastic bats and ravens swayed in the wind. Three jack-o-lanterns glowed eerily in the night.

But Adam only noticed all that in passing. He had more important things to worry about. He couldn't find the doorbell under all the cobwebs, so he knocked frantically. He was surprised to be greeted by what sounded like Sapphie barking.

"Ahh-ha-ha-ha," Cassandra cackled when she opened the door. Dressed as a purple witch in a long, flowing gossamer cape, she wore a standard witch's dress and a purple pointed hat. "When shall we three meet again?" she asked. "In thunder, lightning, or in—"

"Not now," Adam panted.

Belle came to the door behind Cassandra. She was dressed as a red witch. And in her hands, she held Sapphie, who now wore a black and orange scarf tied around her neck.

"I was *wondering* when you'd get here," Belle said, making her voice sound scratchy and deep—the way a witch would.

Cassandra cleared her throat. She waved her hands in the air and chanted. "Double, double, toil and trouble. Cauldron burn and fire bubble..."

Adam was dumbstruck. He kept looking back at the road, but the white van was nowhere to be seen. Then he looked from Sapphie to Belle to Cassandra, wondering how his sister's dog had ended up here again. And why was Cassandra chanting like this? Was she making a spell? Did it have anything to do with the white van? Everything was happening so quickly, he couldn't find any words. His bottom lip trembled.

"We don't have time for this," Patrick said, pushing past Adam. He pulled Adam inside, closing the door behind him.

Belle and Cassandra looked at each other with concern.

Inside, Patrick plopped down on the stairs.

"We can go sit in the living room, if you're tired," Cassandra suggested.

But before anyone could answer, Patrick started crying. Adam had never seen his best friend cry before, and he wasn't sure what to do. Adam tried hard to keep himself from crying, too.

"What's wrong?" Cassandra asked.

Patrick tried to explain through his sobs, but he only managed to point to the door and say "white van" and "kidnap."

Belle and Cassandra looked at Adam. All he could do was nod.

"I think we should call the police," Adam said, and he quickly explained the white van that had tried to kidnap them.

Cassandra called immediately.

"The police said they already have a car coming to this area. There were multiple reports of a white van driving erratically. They should be here any second now."

"Should we call my parents?" Adam asked.

Belle looked out the window toward Adam's house. "Cassandra, look," she whispered.

Cassandra joined her at the window. They looked especially suspicious in their witch's costumes, pointing out the window with their flowing costumes swaying in the draft.

"Should we call my parents?" Adam asked again.

Belle cleared her throat.

"Let's wait until the police get here," Cassandra said. "They'll want you to tell them exactly what happened before you forget."

Adam looked skeptically at Patrick. But they didn't have time to discuss their suspicions before the doorbell rang. It was Officer Dunlap.

"Good evening," he said calmly. He looked around. "Adam Hollinger? Is that you?"

Adam nodded.

"I almost didn't recognize you in your space costume," Officer Dunlap said. "And I *never* would have expected to be here again with you, at this same house."

Adam nodded. "Me either."

He thought back to the summer, when Officer Dunlap had helped after Mr. Frostburg locked Sapphie and Zeph in the shed with all his stolen goods.

Belle still held Sapphie, who caught the scent of Officer Dunlap. She began to bark and bark and squirm until she jumped free of Belle's arms. She ran up to the policeman, nuzzling his leg.

"Good to see you again," he said, patting the dog. "And Zeph is here with you, too?"

"Not Zeph, sir," Adam said. "That's Sapphie, my sister's dog. Zeph was afraid of my costume, so he had to stay home."

"I see," the officer said. "Now, what seems to be the problem?"

By now, Patrick had calmed down enough to help Adam tell the story.

"We were trick-or-treating," Adam began. "And we were just on our way home…"

"We had been seeing this crazy white van all night," Patrick said.

"Crazy white van?" Officer Dunlap asked. He jotted something down on his notepad. "Can you describe it?"

"It was kind of new," Adam said.

"And it was driving all weird," Patrick added. "Like swerving and skidding. It almost hit us."

"Yeah," Adam said. "If we hadn't of jumped onto the grass."

"And what else?" the officer asked.

"The van stopped, and the driver told us to get in," Patrick said. His voice was getting all shaky again, and it seemed like he might cry.

"What did the driver look like?" Officer Dunlap asked.

"He was wearing a ski mask," Adam said. "But it was definitely a male voice."

"And what exactly did he say?"

"He told us to get in," Adam said. "And then the side door to the van opened, and he pointed at it, like we were supposed to get inside."

"And what happened then?"

"We dropped all our candy," Adam said. "We ran up here as fast as we could. The van followed us for a while, but by the time Belle and Cassandra answered the door, we looked and the van was gone."

Cassandra slipped out of the room. Only Adam seemed to notice.

Officer Dunlap nodded. "Well, you did the right thing, staying away and getting an adult to help you."

"Do you have any idea who the man might have been? Could it have been someone you know? Or was it a stranger?" Belle asked.

"He had a mask," Adam said again. "I didn't recognize him."

"I want to call my dad," Patrick said.

Officer Dunlap nodded to Belle.

"Phone's in the kitchen," she said.

"Can I call my parents, too?" Adam asked.

Belle looked at the police officer. "Not yet," she blurted out strangely. "We need more information from you."

"Do we?" the policeman asked.

"Yes," she insisted. "Adam, think. What would your favorite detective do?"

Adam thought what Riley Couth might do in such a situation.

"Anyone suspicious?" Belle suggested. "Maybe someone you've suspected for a while now, but haven't been able to tell on?"

Adam nodded. He was so upset by recent events. He was scared. He was tired. He was nervous about tomorrow's baseball game and the Harvest Dance and fighting with Marnie, and Courtney threatening him. But there was one worry besides all that—a worry he hadn't told to anyone except Patrick. And the fact that Belle wasn't letting him call his father—and that Cassandra had just disappeared—only confirmed his suspicions. Adam's fear hardened into anger, and he pointed a finger at Belle.

"There is someone like that," Adam said. "You."

Belle's jaw dropped.

"What do you mean, Adam?" Officer Dunlap asked.

Adam began. "First of all, we know you're a real witch. You and Cassandra. With your fortune-telling cards and your weird clothing, and Cassandra's weird chanting. You can't fool us anymore."

Officer Dunlap looked at Belle, but neither one said anything. Adam continued.

"I raked leaves for her," Adam said. "And I bagged them up. And the next time I came back to rake leaves, she had dumped them back out onto her yard. I found the paper bag I'd put the leaves in. It was wrinkled and stuffed behind a tree."

"Is this true?" Officer Dunlap asked.

"I—I can explain," Belle offered.

But Adam didn't let her begin. "And when I was raking, she had this purple notebook. She kept asking me questions and watching me. Every so often she'd write something down. It's like she's spying on me. Spying so she can put a spell on me."

Officer Dunlap shook his head. "Adam," he said. "You've been through a lot lately. With Mister Frostburg and your baseball and now tonight—"

"I know what I'm talking about," Adam said.

"It's also Halloween," Officer Dunlap offered. "The imagination tends to run wild at such times."

"How do you explain the fact that Sapphie is here?" Adam asked.

"I assumed she came with you, Adam," Officer Dunlap said.

"No," Adam insisted. "When we rang the doorbell, Belle answered and Sapphie was in her arms."

"I can explain," Belle said.

"And she put a spell on this space costume she gave me so that Zeph would be too scared to go trick-or-treating with me. That way, he wouldn't be around to protect me and Patrick."

"Adam? How could I put a spell on your costume? And even if I could, why on earth would I do that?" Belle asked sadly.

"Besides, Adam," the officer said, "these all sound like coincidences."

"No," Adam said.

He ran into the den. Officer Dunlap followed. Adam searched the coffee table until he found the folder of newspaper clippings. He thrust it into Officer Dunlap's hands.

"If she's not spying on me, then how do you explain *this*?"

Officer Dunlap flipped through the folder.

"Hmm," he said. "Maybe we *should* let Belle do some explaining."

Just then, Patrick and Cassandra came into the room.

"My dad's on his way," Patrick said, sniffling.

"Patrick," Adam said boldly, "I've told Officer Dunlap that these two are witches."

"We're not witches," Belle said. "I was just about to explain."

She sat down on the couch. Adam and Patrick stood together. Officer Dunlap and Cassandra took chairs from the fortune-telling table and sat.

"There's no explaining all the weird stuff I just told you," Adam insisted again. "And besides, why won't you let me call my parents?"

"Adam," Belle said softly. "There's an explanation for all those things."

Adam crossed his arms.

"First of all, I'm not a witch."

"Are you spying on me?" Adam asked.

"No," Belle said. Everyone looked at the folder of articles that Officer Dunlap now held in his hands. "Well," Belle admitted, "maybe just a little."

"I knew it," Adam said. "Why?"

"There's a reason I rented this house," Belle said. She took a deep breath before continuing. "See, the reason I'm going to college is I'm studying psychology. I'm writing my thesis paper, which I hope to get published, on animal and human interaction. When I heard about you and Zeph, and how you discovered Mister Frostburg burglarizing homes, I thought you'd be a perfect case study."

"Case study?" Adam asked.

"Yes," Belle explained. "A perfect example of what I'm studying. That's why I have all these articles about you. It's research."

"Research?" Adam cried. "Like I'm a lab rat in some weird science experiment?" He looked at Patrick. Patrick was so amazed that he had stopped crying. "Does that mean you dumped out all those leaves I raked?"

Belle blushed. "Yes."

"Why?"

"Because I wanted an excuse to spend more time with you. To ask you questions and watch you interact with Zeph."

"So you made me do extra yard work?"

"That's not right," Patrick said. "You could have made him sore for his pitching."

"I'm sorry," Belle said. "It was wrong of me to dump out those leaves after you spent so long raking them." She looked Adam right in the eye.

"But I didn't want you to know you were being studied."

Patrick raised a brow. "If this is all true, then how do you explain Cassandra's weird chanting?"

"And wearing a cloak all the time," Adam said. "And disappearing just now."

Cassandra cleared her throat. "Sorry," she said. "I get overly-enthusiastic sometimes."

"Enthusiastic about what?"

"I'm an actress," she said. "I study theater at the college. We're getting ready to perform *That Scottish Play*," she said. "You know, the famous one."

"*That Scottish Play*?" Adam said. "I've never heard of it."

"It's called *MacBeth*," Belle explained. "But actors are superstitious and won't ever say the name of the play."

"What's that have to do with Cassandra chanting all the time?"

"Double, double, toil and trouble. Fire burn and cauldron bubble," Cassandra chanted, laughing. "See, I'm just rehearsing my lines. I play one of the witches."

"So it was just acting?" Patrick asked.

Cassandra nodded. "Sorry I scared you. I just get overly excited sometimes."

"Why would you wear a cape, then?" Adam asked.

"Just getting used to it," Cassandra said. Her cheeks reddened. "It's easy to trip over, so I thought if I wore it around the house, I'd get used to it in time for the play."

Patrick nodded, but Adam's eyes still flashed with anger.

"Why did you disappear just now?" Adam asked. "How do we know you weren't putting a spell on us?"

Cassandra hurried back to the entryway. "I was finding these," she said, emerging with Adam and Patrick's bags of candy. "When you mentioned that you dropped your candy near our house, I thought I would find it for you. You know, one less thing for the two of you to worry about."

Adam frowned. He felt bad now for accusing Cassandra when she had only been trying to help.

"Here," Cassandra said, grabbing an envelope from the counter. "They give all the actors tickets to the dress rehearsal. I'd like it if you and Patrick, and your families, came along." She handed Adam a stack of tickets.

"See," Belle said. "There's an explanation for everything."

"Why couldn't you have just told me all this?" Adam asked Belle. "It would have been a lot less creepy than you sitting there writing notes about me in your purple notebook. It's why I thought you were a witch."

"I thought that if I told you I was studying you," Belle explained, "you might act differently. It's a thing I learned in school called *observation bias*. People behave differently when they know they're being watched."

"Like Courtney," Adam said. "She acts all nice when people are watching..."

Everyone was silent for a moment. Arabella paused as if deciding whether or not to say something. Finally, she said softly, "Your parents thought it would be best if I didn't tell you, either."

"My parents?" Adam demanded. "They're in on this? They knew you were writing about me?"

"That's why they invited me over to dinner, and to your baseball game. It's why they encouraged you to agree to rake leaves in my backyard."

Adam couldn't believe it. How could his parents go behind his back like that?

"Speaking of my parents," Adam said finally. "There's one more question you never answered."

Belle looked at Cassandra. Both girls turned to Officer Dunlap.

"How come you wouldn't let me call my parents just now?"

Officer Dunlap was the one who answered. "If I may," he said. "As I was coming to answer your call, we got another call on the radio. The white van has been spotted and pulled over. I passed by on my way over here, and I saw someone get out of the back of the van and take off a ski mask. I think Belle and Cassandra didn't want you to see who it was."

"Why?" Adam asked. "Who was it?"

"It was..." Officer Dunlap cleared his throat. "Well, it was... your sister."

"Courtney?" Adam asked.

"Yes," Officer Dunlap said. "It seems she was in the white van when it pulled over to scare you."

Adam nodded. "She told me she was going to scare me during trick-or-treating."

"Looks like she did," Officer Dunlap said.

"When we looked at your driveway," Belle explained, "we saw a police car, and we didn't want to upset you more than you already were. That's why we wanted you to wait before calling your parents."

"If you're not a witch, then how come Sapphie always ends up at your house?"

Belle shrugged. "She's just a good escape artist, I guess. Courtney needs to keep a better eye on her." Belle picked up the puppy and handed her to Adam. "I'm pretty sure she's got a hole dug under your fence."

"You've got good neighbors, Adam," Office Dunlap said. "They certainly look out for you." He nodded to the girls. "Let's get you home." He led the way out the front door, and walked down the driveway and across the street, followed by Patrick, Belle, Cassandra, and Adam, who carried Sapphie.

~ THIRTY-ONE ~
The End of Lies

When Adam got home, Courtney was seated on the family room couch. Her eyes were red and her cheeks were stained with tears. Another police officer, Officer Davies, stood behind the couch with a notepad. When Adam entered the room, his parents both turned to him, as did the police officer. Only Courtney kept her eyes to the ground.

"He was at the old Frostburg house," Officer Dunlap explained. "He ran there after the white minivan attempted to kidnap him."

Mrs. Hollinger ran to Adam, hugging him tightly. Sapphie squirmed. "I'm fine, Mom," Adam said angrily. "Sapphie was over at Belle's house."

Mrs. Hollinger gave Adam a strange look, wondering why he seemed angry.

Belle smiled sheepishly. "I told Adam about my research project," she said. "I guess we should have told him earlier."

Mrs. Hollinger smiled. "We'll talk about it later, okay?" She turned to Mr. Hollinger. "If Sapphie got loose from the backyard, I wonder if Zeph got loose, too."

"I'll check," Adam gasped and put Sapphie on the floor.

Sapphie yelped and ran immediately to Courtney. She jumped into her lap and sniffed her face curiously. Sapphie let out a few squeals before licking the tears from Courtney's face.

"No, Adam," Mrs. Hollinger said. "You need to stay here."

"I'll check for you, Adam," Belle said.

Patrick stood nervously in the corner of the room. Cassandra stood with him. "I called my dad," he said.

Mrs. Hollinger nodded. "Courtney was just telling us what happened," she said. "Both of you, Adam and Patrick, need to hear this. Courtney, I think you'd better explain to your brother."

Just then, Coach Harris entered through the front door. He hugged Patrick, who still seemed to be fighting tears.

"What's going on here?" Coach Harris asked. Adam had never seen him so serious, not even during their worst games.

"Courtney was just about to explain," Mrs. Hollinger said.

Courtney put Sapphie on the ground. Sapphie looked at her indignantly, as if to ask how anyone could ignore such a cute puppy. But the look on Courtney's face made Sapphie crawl over to Zeph's rocket ship bed, curl up, and watch the situation through half-closed lids.

Courtney took a few uneven breaths before she spoke.

"It was me in that minivan," Courtney said finally. "I was the one who opened the van's door to scare you."

"Who was driving?" Adam asked.

"JJ."

"That was your plan all along? To pretend to kidnap us?"

Courtney sniffled again. "We were hoping you'd get into the van."

"Why?"

"We were dressed like kidnappers, Meghan and I. All in black with masks and everything. We were going to blindfold you and scare you until you revealed embarrassing secrets. Meghan had a video camera, and we were going to film it and post it online."

Adam didn't know what to say. Ever since she got to middle school, Courtney had been mean to him. But this was worse than he ever imagined she could be.

"I guess I shouldn't expect your forgiveness," Courtney said.

"Give him time, Courtney," Mr. Hollinger said. "This was a rotten thing to do."

"The worst thing you've ever done," Mrs. Hollinger added.

"The worst part," Officer Davies explained, "is that JJ isn't even old enough to drive. He took his mother's keys, stole the minivan, and took it for a joyride. Did some damage to the car, too—running it up onto the side of the road. Hitting a mailbox or two." Officer Davies turned to Courtney. "And you and Meghan were in the back of the van with no seatbelts. You're lucky all JJ hit was a mailbox."

"I'm sorry," Courtney muttered.

"JJ's going to be in serious trouble for this," Officer Davies explained. "As for you and Meghan, I'd expect you to be assigned some community service. And I'm sure your parents will have something for you as well in the way of punishment."

Courtney looked first at her mom, then her dad. "Here," she said, giving them her cell phone. "I already know you're going to take it away."

Mr. Hollinger nodded. He took the cell phone, removed the battery, and put it in his pocket.

"How long have you been hanging out with this JJ fellow?" Mr. Hollinger asked. "You never once mentioned him until we caught you wearing his jacket at that baseball game."

"Adam knew the whole time," Courtney mumbled.

"You shouldn't have kept JJ a secret," Mrs. Hollinger said. "Neither you, nor Adam."

"It wasn't right of you to hide information from me, either," Adam said angrily. "You should have told me about Belle." The more Adam spoke, the more upset he became. "Besides, Courtney and JJ threatened me. They threatened me if I told on them. And they made me walk home by myself the other day, and—" It was too much. Now it was Adam who started crying.

As soon as Courtney saw her brother cry, she broke into another round of sobs. Mrs. Hollinger, upset about both children, started to cry.

There was a knock on the door, and another police officer entered, and escorted JJ inside. JJ was wearing handcuffs, his hands held awkwardly behind his back. As soon as he stepped into the room, Courtney's eyes lit up.

"Sorry for the further disturbance," the officer said. "JJ has something he wanted to say."

JJ turned to Adam. "I'm sorry I scared you." He turned to Patrick. "Sorry," he said again. He didn't look sorry, but he sure looked scared.

"Why did you do it?" Mrs. Hollinger asked.

"I was just bored, I guess," JJ said.

"Bored?" Mrs. Hollinger shook her head in disbelief. "And you, Courtney? Why did you do it?"

Courtney turned red, and a few more tears dripped down her cheek. "I just wanted JJ to like me. I was going to the high school homecoming dance with him."

JJ's eyes bulged open. "No you weren't," he said.

"I wasn't?" Courtney asked. "But I thought, since we hung out so much?"

JJ shook his head. "Why would I take a seventh grader to a high school dance? I already have a date. Had one, I guess. There'll be no homecoming dance for me now. How could you ever think I'd take someone the same age as my sister to a high school dance?" JJ thought about it a moment, then laughed.

Courtney sobbed more passionately than before.

"Get him out of our house," Mr. Hollinger said.

The officer nodded and escorted JJ out.

"Time for us to go, too," Coach Harris said. "We've got our big game tomorrow against Altoona. Adam, Patrick, I know it's been a tough night, but you need to rest up. The Angels are the toughest team in the league. They've been undefeated for years now."

"After a night like this," Adam said, "playing the toughest team in the league doesn't seem all that scary."

Coach Harris nodded and led Patrick out the front door.

~ * ~

Cassandra cleared her throat. "I guess I should be going, too." She said goodnight and followed Patrick out the door.

"You two," Mr. Hollinger said to Adam and Courtney. "Up to bed."

Adam nodded just as Belle was coming in from the back yard, and she looked pale as a ghost.

"There's a hole under your fence. It must have been how Sapphie got out... but now Zeph is gone."

~ THIRTY-TWO ~
Sibling Sympathy

"I've got to help look for him," Adam sobbed.

"You need to take a nice hot shower," Mr. Hollinger insisted. "You've had enough for one night. You and Courtney stay here, and your mom and I, and Belle and Cassandra, will take Sapphie and try to find Zeph."

"Try?" Adam gasped.

"Find him," Mr. Hollinger corrected.

"How can I take a shower when Zeph is out there all by himself?" Adam sobbed.

But the look on Mr. Hollinger's face told Adam that his pleas were useless. Reluctantly, Adam trudged upstairs and turned on the shower. As the warm water fogged up the bathroom, Adam wrote Zeph's name on the steamy mirror and hoped he'd be found quickly.

After his shower, Adam threw on a towel and ran into the hallway. His hair was dripping wet. "Zeph?" he called.

"They're not back yet," Courtney said. She sat on her bed, hugging a pillow. Her breathing was unsteady, as if she might start crying again.

"Oh," Adam said. He turned his back on her, went into his room, and closed the door.

A moment later, Courtney knocked.

"What do you want?" Adam asked.

"Can I come in?" Courtney asked.

Adam stepped out in his pajamas. His hair was still wet and disheveled. "What do you want?" he demanded.

"I'm really sorry," Courtney said. For the first time, she seemed like she meant it.

"This was the worst thing you've ever done," Adam said. He looked at the clock. It was already almost 10:00. "I was supposed to get to bed early. I have my most important game tomorrow."

"I know," Courtney said. "It was rotten of me."

"I don't understand you," Adam said. "Sometimes I don't even know how we're related. How could you do something like this?"

"I thought JJ liked me," Courtney said. "I thought he was going to take me to his high school's homecoming dance."

Adam rolled his eyes.

"Speaking of dances," Adam said. "And you'd *better* be honest with me after all that's happened. Why does Marnie want me to go to the Harvest Dance with her? What kind of trick are you all planning for me?"

Courtney shook her head. "There's no trick, Adam," she promised.

"How can I possibly believe you? You wanted to make a fool out of me by pretending to kidnap me. Now you want to make a fool out of me by sending me to the dance with Marnie."

Courtney shook her head again, fighting tears. "I know how it feels to have my heart broken," Courtney said, "and I don't want Marnie to feel the same way. The only reason she wants you to go the Harvest Dance with her is that she likes you."

"Eww," Adam said.

"Adam," Courtney scolded. "She's a nice girl."

Adam frowned.

"That's why she threw sand at those other girls. She was jealous."

Adam nodded.

"So are you going to the dance with her?"

"It depends on my game," Adam said. "If we tie during the first two games, we're going to have to play a third."

"Well," Courtney said, "whatever the case may be, don't turn out to be like JJ."

Adam nodded.

"You know, I can see why Marnie would like you."

"Huh?" Adam asked.

"Even though you're kind of dorky, you *are* smart, and you're good at baseball, and you're a pretty nice guy. Not like JJ," she sniffled.

Adam could barely believe his sister was complimenting him. He felt his ears start to burn just as the front door opened.

"Zeph?" Adam shouted.

Zeph barked and bounded up the stairs, taking a running leap into Adam's arms.

"Zeph, Zeph," Adam shouted. "Where were you?"

"We searched everywhere," Mrs. Hollinger said.

"But it turns out he was in my backyard," Belle said. "He must have followed Sapphie's scent, and he must have been waiting for her and ended up falling asleep, curled up in the leaf pile."

Adam hugged his puppy and turned to Belle. "I'm sorry I thought you were a witch," Adam said. "I hope you can forgive me."

"It's already in the past," Belle said. "You should get to bed. Goodnight and good luck at your game."

"I'll wear your good luck charm," Adam said.

When Mr. and Mrs. Hollinger went upstairs to bed later that evening, they saw that Zeph had fallen asleep curled up at the foot of Adam's bed. While they didn't normally allow the puppies to sleep in the bedroom, Adam and Zeph looked so peaceful that they allowed it—just this once.

~ THIRTY-THREE ~
Repercussions

Adam felt exhausted the next morning at school. Worse, the first person Adam saw when his mom dropped him off was Marnie Ellison.

Adam lowered his eyes to the ground and tried to speed past her. All he needed after the events of last night was Marnie acting weird again. Most importantly, he didn't want to talk to her about the Harvest Dance. What if Courtney was right? What if Marnie *did* have a crush on him? It was the last thing he wanted to deal with just then.

But despite Adam's best efforts, Marnie ran over to him as quickly as she could.

"Adam," she called.

Adam tried to ignore her.

"Adam," she called again.

Adam turned around, but instead of seeing Marnie, he saw Olivia and Amira running toward him.

"Adam," Olivia called. "Isn't today your big game?"

"We heard you get to leave school early to-day. How exciting," Amira added.

"Did you think about the Harvest Dance at all?" Olivia asked.

They each stood on one side of Adam.

"I..." Adam was so exhausted and frazzled that he didn't know what to say.

"I *told* you he doesn't want to go with you," Marnie shouted, pushing her way between Adam and Olivia. "Besides, he's going to the Harvest Dance with *me*, so scram."

"Is that true, Adam?" Amira asked. Her voice sounded sad, and Adam felt terrible. Still, he didn't want to act like JJ, who hurt Courtney's feelings by not telling her the truth.

"It's true," Adam said.

Olivia and Amira frowned, turned on their heels with a huff, and marched off into the school.

Adam turned to Marnie.

Marnie smiled. "We *are* going together, right?"

Adam shrugged. "I have three games against the Altoona Angels."

"Two games, if you lose," Marnie added.

Adam gave her a dirty look.

"Sorry," she said. "It's just, well, everyone's heard the Angels' reputation. They haven't lost a game in three years."

"Yep, they're pretty good."

"Not that I want you to lose," Marnie said, blushing, "but I hope you get to go to the dance."

Adam rolled his eyes.

"My sister said she's been trying to text message Courtney all night," Marnie said. "But Courtney isn't responding. Courtney was supposed to be hanging out with Meghan and JJ last night. Aileen was supposed to go too, but my parents found out and made her stay home. Aileen was worried that something happened."

Adam rolled his eyes again.

"Did something happen?" Marnie asked.

Adam sat on a concrete bench in the courtyard, and Marnie sat next to him. Adam wondered why she couldn't sit on the bench opposite him, instead.

"Courtney, Meghan, and JJ stole JJ's parents' minivan," Adam explained. "JJ was driving."

"Oh," Marnie said.

"They pretended to be kidnappers. They were dressed up in dark clothes and face masks. They followed me and Patrick and tried to get us to come along with them."

"What happened?" Marnie asked.

"We ran to a neighbor's house and called the cops. They eventually caught the van and JJ was arrested." The more Adam talked about it, the more tired he felt. He couldn't believe something like that had actually happened to him.

"Was Courtney arrested? And Meghan?"

"No. They have to go to court and probably do community service. And my parents took away her cell phone."

"For how long?"

"Probably forever," Adam said. "I've never seen Mom and Dad so mad."

Marnie shook her head. "I guess it's a good thing that Aileen wasn't allowed to go with them."

Adam shrugged. "Now that Courtney's probably going to be grounded forever, Aileen will just have more time to help you torment me."

Marnie frowned. Without warning, she hopped off the bench and dashed into the school, leaving Adam sitting all alone.

~ * ~

Adam and Patrick were allowed to leave school during recess. Coach Harris would drive them to Altoona, where they would prepare for their afternoon game. Then, they'd stay in a hotel to be ready for Saturday morning's game. A third game, if necessary, was scheduled for Saturday afternoon.

Mrs. Patterson, the school's secretary, came out to the recess field to find Adam and Patrick.

"Boys," she said, "Mr. Harris is here to take you to your game."

Adam and Patrick had been watching the dodge ball game. Now, they looked at each other nervously.

"Don't be nervous, boys," Mrs. Patterson said. "You'll do great. We're all cheering for you."

Patrick and Adam followed Mrs. Patterson, but Marnie stopped Adam just before he went inside.

"Wait," she said.

"What is it?" Adam asked impatiently.

"Good luck," she said.

"Thanks."

Marnie stood awkwardly.

"Anything else?" Adam asked. Patrick had already gone inside, and Adam didn't want to keep Coach Harris waiting.

"If you *do* come to the Harvest Dance, where should I meet you?"

"I don't know," Adam said.

"I'll wait for you outside, then," Marnie said.

"You're not allowed to be outside by yourself," Adam said.

Marnie smiled. "I'll find a way."

"Okay." Adam shrugged.

Still, Marnie stood awkwardly staring at Adam.

"Anything else?" Adam asked again.

"Well," Marnie said. "If we're going to the dance together, we should make sure our costumes match."

"Why?"

"So everyone'll know we're going together."

Adam felt his ears start to redden.

"What are you going as?" Marnie asked. "I know you don't have time to plan a new costume because of your game. But if you tell me what you're going as, maybe I can find a costume to match."

"If I make it to the dance, I'll be coming back from the game. So, I guess I'll just go in my baseball uniform."

"Your red one?" Marnie asked.

Adam nodded.

"I'm sure I'll be able to figure out *something* to wear. Besides, now that Courtney's grounded, Aileen will have time to help me."

"Whatever you say," Adam muttered, and pushed past her into the school.

"Good luck," Marnie called to him.

~ * ~

The car ride to the game seemed like it lasted forever. Adam and Patrick were tired from the night before. Neither of them slept very well. On top of that, they were nervous about playing the best team in the league.

"I had nightmares all last night," Patrick admitted as his dad drove down the highway. "I was being chased by a white van driven by a jack-o-lantern."

Adam nodded.

"Did you have any bad dreams?" Patrick asked.

"Not that I remember. At least your nightmares go away when you wake up," Adam said. "Marnie follows me during all my waking hours."

"Marnie? Why?"

"She was bothering me at recess today. She still wants to go to that Harvest Dance with me. She was bugging me about what costume I'm going in."

"Why?" Patrick asked.

"She wants to find a costume to match mine. I don't understand her. All year she was tormenting me. She would tease me in front of the whole class. Throw things at me. Make fun of me. And now she wants to wear a costume that matches mine. Part of me thinks she wants to play another prank on me."

From the front seat, Coach Harris chuckled. "I don't think she's gonna play a trick on you, Adam," he said.

"How do you know?"

"When girls have a crush on guys, they sometimes have weird ways of getting the guy's attention," Coach Harris explained.

"Like throwing things at me?" Adam asked.

"And acting weird in front of other girls?" Patrick added.

"Exactly," Coach Harris said. "Adam, if you do end up going to the dance, just be nice to her. If you are, her strange behavior should change from now on."

Adam nodded. "It's worth a try, I guess."

The car grew silent. The boys' minds shifted focus from girls to the game.

"You think what Cassandra told us will come true?" Patrick asked.

"You mean when she told your fortune?" Adam asked.

"Yes."

"What fortune was that?" Coach Harris asked.

Adam gasped. "Patrick, what did she tell you about a big white thing, again?" he asked, ignoring Coach Harris.

"She said beware of something big and white." Patrick's eyes opened wide. "Adam, her fortune came true!"

"The big white van!"

Coach Harris cleared his throat. "What fortune, boys?"

Patrick explained. "Adam's neighbor, Belle. She said we'd play our best, and we'd be proud of our performance, but she didn't say we'd win. In fact, the look in her eyes made it seem like—"

"Seem like what?" Coach Harris asked.

"Made it seem like we wouldn't win today."

Coach Harris offered a smile through the rear-view mirror. "In any case," he said, "she gave you some good advice. The Angels are a tough team to beat. We should be proud we've made it this far."

Adam nodded. "And what was the third prediction?"

"Something about a masquerade," Patrick said.

Adam felt his ears burn. "You mean like the Halloween parade at the Harvest Dance?"

The car was silent for a while. Adam was hoping to change the subject. "I sure hope the dogs are okay," he said.

"Why? Where are they staying while your parents are here at the game?"

"They're staying at home," Adam said. "Mom got Belle to stay overnight and dog-sit them."

Patrick laughed. "Good thing we know she's not a witch," he said.

"Yeah," Adam said. He tried to laugh, but he couldn't help the knot that was getting tighter and tighter in his stomach.

~ * ~

Mr. and Mrs. Hollinger had originally planned on watching Adam's game on Friday, staying over in the hotel, and driving home after the end of the tournament on Saturday. Originally, they had planned on allowing Courtney to stay overnight at Aileen's house. After the events of Halloween, however, they decided that Courtney was coming with them.

She sat miserably in the back of the minivan while her parents listened to old-people music. When they got to the game, they bought tickets, and Mrs. Hollinger and Courtney found seats while Mr. Hollinger bought some snacks.

After she sat down in the bleachers, Courtney rolled her eyes. "Why are we even here?" she asked. "The Lancaster Reds have no chance."

She pointed to the Altoona Angels. They were dressed in dark green uniforms, and every member of the team looked tall and muscular.

Mrs. Hollinger eyed the other team skeptically. "They *do* look large for their age," she said.

"They train all year for this," Mr. Hollinger said. "I overheard some of the Angels' parents over at the snack bar. They lift weights and have private coaches."

Courtney rolled her eyes again. "What's the point?" she asked. "If they're that good, they should just win. And then we can leave this stupid game."

Mr. and Mrs. Hollinger crossed their arms and looked angrily at Courtney.

"After what you did on Halloween, I can't believe you still have such an attitude," Mrs. Hollinger said.

"You need to get serious," Mr. Hollinger agreed.

"In fact, maybe this is a good time to talk about your punishment," Mrs. Hollinger said.

"My punishment?" Courtney asked.

"You heard the officer. When you go for your court date, you'll likely be sentenced to community service."

Courtney stuck out her tongue. "That sounds so stupid."

"Be thankful, young lady, that you didn't end up arrested like JJ," Mr. Hollinger said.

"Hmph," Courtney muttered.

"We were thinking about what community service would best suit you," Mrs. Hollinger said. "We were also thinking about Sapphie and how you seem to have been neglecting her. She's a rambunctious little dog, and she needs a lot more attention than you've been giving her."

Courtney shrugged.

"I've signed you up to volunteer at Willow Lakes," Mrs. Hollinger said.

"The *nursing home?*" Courtney scowled.

"Yes, the nursing home," Mrs. Hollinger said. "The residents there are lonely. They could really benefit from you visiting."

"How could you sign me up? The judge hasn't even told me how many hours I have to do for community service."

"It doesn't matter. We want you to start volunteering as soon as possible." Mrs. Hollinger looked at her husband. "And *we'll* tell you when you've completed enough hours."

"Also," Mr. Hollinger added, "the residents at Willow Lakes often appreciate animal visits."

"Animal visits?" Courtney asked.

"Yes. Like from a puppy," Mr. Hollinger said.

"A puppy?"

"I've signed you and Sapphie up for obedience classes once a week. While you're there, you need to heed the instructor. After class, you need to practice what you've learned with Sapphie."

"That sounds like homework," Courtney moaned.

"It'll be good for the both of you," Mr. Hollinger said.

"How come Adam doesn't have to go with Zeph?" Courtney asked.

"Adam takes good care of Zeph," Mrs. Hollinger said.

Courtney crossed her arms. "Fine," she whispered. "I just hope these Angels are as good as they look. Then the game will be over before we know it."

~ THIRTY-FOUR ~
Angels at Attention

The Lancaster Reds sat in the dugout watching the Altoona Angels warm up. Even Adam felt there was no chance at winning.

"They're just too good," Adam said.

"They look like seventh-graders," Patrick added.

"Now, boys," Coach Harris said. "Let's be proud that we're here. Even if the Angels are the best, there's one team in the league that's good enough to play them, and that's us. Let's play our best and be proud of our performance. Let's have no *should-have's* or *could-have's*."

The boys nodded.

"Let's play," Coach Harris yelled. "One, two, three..."

"Reds," the team shouted in unison.

Greg was first at bat. He stood at the plate with muscles tensed. He looked ready to hit the ball out of the park. But the first two pitches were so fast that Greg didn't even have time to swing.

"Strike," the umpire called twice in a row.

"We're in trouble," Patrick told Adam. "You'd better get used to the idea of going to that dance with Marnie. At this rate, we'll lose in about twelve minutes."

Adam took a deep breath. "Patrick, I—"

"Adam. Patrick. Focus. Patrick, you're on deck," Coach Harris yelled.

After missing the first two pitches, Greg swung at the third. The third pitch was slower and a little high. Greg made contact, but not solid contact. The ball flew into the air, and the catcher hustled out of the batter's box to snatch it.

"Out!" the umpire yelled.

On the large light-up board, a "1" appeared next to the out box.

"You're up, Patrick," Adam said. "Good luck."

Patrick swung at the first pitch. He hit a line-drive right at the pitcher. The pitcher scooped it out of the air like it was nothing.

"Out!" the umpire yelled again.

"I wish I could do that," Adam mumbled, remembering the last time he was almost slammed in the chest with a line-drive.

"Let's go, Adam," the team cheered as Adam walked to the plate. Adam swung twice, missing each time. The third time, he made contact with the ball and hit one all the way to the end of the field. He ran as fast as he could, pulling a triple out of the hit.

"Nice hit, Adam," Coach called. "Alex, bring him home!"

Alex was a strong hitter. Of all the players, he was best at aiming hits. He surveyed the field as he stepped up to the plate. Adam watched as Alex seemed to find a hole in the field just behind first base. He would aim there. Alex swung on the first pitch, driving a fast ball right behind the first baseman. It was enough to get Randy to first base and Adam home.

"One—zero," Coach Harris called to the boys. "Keep it up."

"You're being careless, Angels," the Angels' coach yelled. "This is ridiculous. End this inning."

As if following his orders, the Angels stood taller. The pitcher threw more slowly, allowing Steven to hit a pop-up, which the outfielders easily caught.

"Three outs," the umpire called.

"Adam, it's all you," Coach Harris said before the boys took the field. "I'm starting with you because you have what it takes. Just throw your best pitches, and let your team do the rest. These boys may have professional coaches, but we have heart. So, let's show them what we've got. Greg," he shouted. "Be ready when Adam gets tired."

Adam and Greg nodded.

Adam's first pitch was a perfect change-up. But the batter hit it anyway. The Reds fumbled with the ball, allowing the Angels to make it to second base.

"They're fast runners," the outfielders mumbled to each other after throwing in the ball.

Adam took his place again. The next batter, number 12, looked especially tough. He glared at Adam, his eyes narrowed into little slits. As Adam wound up, the batter's lips drew up into a smile. He made contact with the ball, sending a line-drive right at Adam.

Adam ducked down, slamming his head into the pitcher's mound. The second baseman picked up the ball and tagged the runner who had been on second.

"One out," the umpire called.

"Hollinger, you all right out there?" Coach Harris yelled.

Adam stood on the pitcher's mound. His hand shook. "I'm fine," Adam yelled, even though he didn't feel fine. He had almost been slammed in the stomach with a ball. His eye pulsed where it had slammed into the pitcher's mound. He imagined it would be red before long.

Adam tried to stop shaking as he threw the next pitch. It was a ball.

"Outside," the umpire called.

"Adam, focus," Coach Harris yelled.

Adam looked into the stands to see his parents, but the seats were so packed, he couldn't tell where they were.

"Hit another line drive," the Angels' coach yelled. "You've got the pitcher spooked!"

Adam watched in horror as the next batter nodded, glared at Adam, and stood poised to bat.

The batter did as his coach asked. He hit another line drive right at Adam. Adam deflected the hit with his glove, sending it back toward the catcher. The catcher ran for the ball, but by then, the batter had already made it to first, sending another runner to second.

"This is going to be a long game," Adam thought, touching the sensitive and swelling skin around his eye.

Adam pitched for another inning, but then Coach Harris sent in Greg. Adam was badly shaken from that first line-drive. He tried to concentrate on what his dad taught him: fastballs, change-ups, breaking balls. But every time he released the ball, he was more focused on ducking out of the way than getting his pitch right.

~ * ~

"Boy," Coach Harris said as Adam rested in the dugout during the seventh inning. "That eye of yours looks like it's going to be a shiner."

"A shiner?" Adam asked.

"You know," Coach Harris explained. "A black eye. You'd better get more ice on it."

Adam brought his hand to his face. The skin around his eye felt warm and puffy. But the pain of his eye wasn't even the worst thing. Adam felt like he was letting down his team. The Reds were hardly scoring any runs, and the Angels were making more than enough.

When the umpire called the final out in the ninth inning, the score was four to twenty. The boys were more relieved that the game was over, than upset that they had lost. They watched as the Angels dumped the cooler of water over their coach despite the cool weather.

Patrick plopped down on the bench next to Adam. "Are you wearing that red necklace Arabella gave you?" he asked.

"No," Adam said. "I decided not to wear it. Why?"

"Maybe you should have been," Patrick said. "Maybe it really it good luck after all."

~ * ~

Back at the hotel, Coach Harris called a meeting in one of the banquet rooms, where the team and family members would be having dinner.

"Well, Reds," he said after everyone had settled in. "We all know the Angels are a tough team to beat. And we all know we have to play them again tomorrow."

The room filled with groans. This was the toughest game the boys had ever played. They couldn't imagine going through it all again in the morning. Adam held an icepack to his eye and slid into his chair.

"I know you're tired," Coach Harris said. "But here's what I saw today. I saw a pitcher scared of the ball. I saw batters intimidated by the Angels' pitcher. I saw outfielders giving up right there on the field, resigning to the fact that the Angels might score a homerun. Am I wrong?"

The boys looked at their feet. They *had* been intimidated by the Angels. It was hard not to be.

"So, here's what I propose," Coach Harris said. "Tomorrow, we have to play the Angels again. We can play them as a scared little team from Lancaster, or we can play them as a proud team that earned the right out of all the teams in Autumn League to be in the final playoffs. I say we play confidently. What do you say?"

It was hard for the boys to get pumped up after such a difficult game. Still, Patrick felt bad for his dad. "I agree," he said.

Some of the boys looked at him hesitantly.

"Me, too," said Greg.

The boys looked at Adam, who was holding a pack of ice over his quickly-darkening eye. "Me too," Adam said.

With that, all the boys stood, and everyone in the room applauded. Adam looked around. He saw his mom and dad standing and clapping. Even Courtney was clapping. Adam smiled, and despite his aching eye, he actually looked forward to tomorrow.

~ THIRTY-FIVE ~
The Second Challenge

On Saturday, Adam rose early with the rest of the boys. He had slept soundly, even in the hotel's lumpy bed. He put on his uniform and opened the door to meet the rest of his team. But he thought of something, and hurried back into his room. He dug through his bags until he found it—the red necklace Arabella had given him. He knew she wasn't a witch, but maybe the necklace was good luck. It sure couldn't hurt.

In the lobby downstairs, all the boys wanted to get a look at Adam's black eye.

"That's so cool," Greg said. "Wait 'til all the kids see it on Monday."

"It'll be a great story to tell," Alex agreed.

Everyone expected Coach Harris to make them warm up before the game. But they found their coach sitting at a table in the banquet room drinking coffee and reading the paper.

"Dad?" Patrick asked. "Shouldn't you be getting ready for warm ups?"

The other boys shuffled in behind Patrick. They were all dressed in fresh uniforms, which some of the parents had volunteered to wash in the hotel's laundry facilities the night before.

A few of the parents, including Mr. and Mrs. Hollinger, shuffled in behind the boys.

Slowly, Coach Harris put down his newspaper. He took a look at the team.

"You guys look real good in your uniforms," he said.

"*Really* good," Mrs. Hollinger corrected in a whisper to her husband.

"And I know that we're ready for today's game. We've been practicing all season. We've made it this far. You know what I think would be better than a warm up?"

"What?" some of the boys asked in unison.

"Breakfast," Coach Harris said. He nodded to one of the hotel waiters, who nodded back and left the room. He entered again a moment later carrying a tray. He was followed by three other waiters carrying similar trays.

The boys took their seats as the waiters served them egg sandwiches and fruit salad. No one, not even Coach, talked about the morning's game. Instead, they talked about school and Halloween, their pets and families and friends.

When the boys finished eating, the room was full of light-hearted chatter.

Coach Harris stood and cleared his throat. "You know what I saw this morning?" he asked no one in particular. The room quieted, and he continued speaking. "I went out to the field and I saw the Angels running laps. I watched them do that for a while. Then I watched them practice hitting. Then fielding. You know what that means?" Coach asked.

No one answered.

"It means they're going to be tired while we're going to be rested."

The boys smiled.

"So have confidence today. No matter what, as long as you play your best, you can be proud."

Adam turned to Patrick. "That sounds familiar," Adam said, thinking about Cassandra's fortune.

Patrick nodded. "You can say that again."

~ * ~

Coach Harris asked Adam to pitch first while he was fresh. Mrs. Hollinger was worried about Adam's eye, and Coach Harris promised to pull Adam out of the game if he seemed too tired or sore. On the pitcher's mound, Coach Harris's words echoed in Adam's mind. Before his first pitch, Adam blocked out all distractions. He stopped worrying about how Zeph was doing with the strange Arabella Spinelli. He stopped worrying about what Marnie was planning for the Harvest Dance tonight. He stopped worrying about Courtney's future plans to torment him, and he stopped wondering how his classmates would react to his black eye on Monday.

He took a deep breath and released his first pitch. It was a perfect fastball. The batter swung and missed.

"Strike one!" the umpire called.

The second pitch was a breaking ball. Adam could imagine his dad watching proudly from the stands. His form was perfect.

"Strike two!" the umpire called.

The third pitch was so fast, the batter didn't even swing.

"You're out!" the umpire called.

Adam turned to look at the stands, where crowds of people cheered—and they were cheering for him. It was going to be a great game.

~ * ~

By the end of the game, Adam was exhausted. And yet he was fully energized. He and Greg had split the pitching for the game, and Adam had never done so well in his life. As he looked at the scoreboard, he couldn't be prouder. The final score: Reds 5, Angels 6. The Reds had lost by only one run.

"Quite an accomplishment, considering our competition," Coach Harris said.

Even the Angels' coach congratulated the team. "You Reds should be proud," he said. "No team has ever come so close to beating us since I've been coaching."

With that, the Reds cheered—and they even dumped the cooler of icy water on Coach Harris.

Adam rode home with his parents and sister. They stopped for burgers on the way.

"Nice job, Adam," Courtney mumbled as they waited for their food.

"Thanks," Adam said.

"That was nice of you, Courtney," Mr. Hollinger said.

"Well, I figure if I'm nice to my brother, maybe you guys won't make me volunteer so much."

"Volunteer?" Adam asked.

Reluctantly, Courtney told Adam about her mandatory volunteer hours at the nursing home and the training class with Sapphie.

"Adam," Mrs. Hollinger said. "It's getting late. If you still want to go to that Harvest Dance, it looks like we're going to have to drop you off at the school on our way back into Stoney Brook."

"But you don't have to go to the dance," Mr. Hollinger suggested. "I understand if you're tired. It's probably best if you just rest and get some more ice on your eye."

Adam thought about the offer. It was tempting just to go home and relax for the rest of the day. Adam could just picture his fluffy bed, a comic book on his lap, and Zeph at his feet.

Courtney leaned in to her brother. "Marnie will be disappointed if you don't make it."

Adam remembered how upset Courtney had been on Halloween after she had her heart set on hanging out with JJ. Adam didn't want Marnie to feel the same way—as much as she tormented him.

"No," Adam said to his father, gathering his courage. "I'd like to go."

~ THIRTY-SIX ~
The Puppies' People

The Hollinger household had been quiet for the past two days. Sapphie didn't like it one bit.

"Where is Courtney, Courtney, *Courtney*?" she asked Zeph.

Zeph sat near the kitchen window, peeking outside every time he heard a noise.

"Probably the same place as Adam."

"Where's that?" Sapphie asked, nuzzling against him.

"I wish I knew."

The two puppies stared out the window for a while.

"Zeph?" Sapphie asked.

"Yes?"

"Is Arabella our new Person?"

Zeph didn't answer.

"I mean, she was here late last night."

"True," said Zeph.

"And she put us to bed."

"Yes."

"And she gave us about a zillion treats."

"Yes."

"And this morning, when I barked and barked for Courtney to let me out of my cage, Courtney didn't answer. Only Arabella did. What do you think, Zeph?"

Zeph hung his head. "Maybe our People disappeared. Maybe Belle is our new Person."

"Zeph?" Sapphie said. "I don't want Arabella to be my new Person. I mean, I like all the scarves she gives me, and she's nice and smells kinda fun, but..."

Zeph sighed. "I know what you mean. There's just something about my Adam. I miss him. I want him back."

"I miss my Courtney, too," Sapphie agreed. "And another thing. Did you see what this Arabella person did last night? While we were playing out back, she filled in my adventure tunnel. The nerve."

"It's for your own good," Zeph said.

"You used the adventure tunnel, too." Sapphie tugged on his ear.

"Only to find you," Zeph said.

"Well, anyway. As soon as Courtney gets back, I'm going to dig, dig, *dig*!"

Zeph stared out the window. "You think they're coming back?" he asked.

But before Sapphie could answer, Belle's friendly voice called from the family room. "Puppies," she said. "Who wants to play outside? I've got tennis balls and squeaky toys and chewies..."

At the mention of their favorite toys, the corgis forgot all about their missing People and skittered down the stairs to join their new friend Belle.

~ THIRTY-SEVEN ~
The Final Challenge

When Adam's parents pulled into the school parking lot, Ms. Wilkerson was standing outside. "Hi there, Adam," she said, marking his name off a list.

Adam stepped out of the car. He was still wearing his uniform, which was covered in dirt. His baseball cap was pulled low over his eyes.

"Patrick's already here," Ms. Wilkerson explained. "I heard you guys did really well at the game. You almost beat those Angels."

"Yeah," Adam muttered. He looked up.

"Oh my," Ms. Wilkerson exclaimed. "What happened to your eye?"

"I had a run-in with the pitching mound," Adam said. "The pitching mound won."

"Have him call us if it bothers him, or if he needs more ice," Mrs. Hollinger said.

Ms. Wilkerson nodded. Adam watched his parents pull away from the curb, up the hill, and down the street.

"Adam," Ms. Wilkerson said. "There's someone who's been waiting for you."

"For me?" Adam asked.

Ms. Wilkerson nodded. She pointed to the courtyard, where a girl dressed in red was sitting on one of the concrete benches.

"Marnie?" Adam asked.

Marnie jumped up and ran toward Adam. She was dressed in a red soccer uniform. It nearly matched Adam's baseball uniform.

"Adam," Marnie said. "What happened to your eye?"

"I bashed into the pitcher's mound dodging a line drive," he said.

"That must have hurt," Marnie said. "Why didn't you just catch it instead of diving into the pitcher's mound?" Marnie asked.

Adam frowned and cast his eyes to the ground.

"Sorry," Marnie said. "I didn't mean that." She cleared her throat. "You didn't have to come to the dance if you didn't want to." She looked down, too.

Adam thought about what Courtney said. About how sad Courtney had been when JJ broke her heart. "No," he told Marnie. "I wanted to come."

Marnie's face stretched into a big smile.

"Adam," she said.

"Yes?"

"I'm sorry I was so mean to you."

Adam shrugged.

"I guess I just wanted to be your friend," she said. "But I was afraid my sister and your sister would make fun of me."

Adam nodded. "I don't think we should care what either of them think about us." He didn't know what else to say.

Ms. Wilkerson said, "You two should get inside now."

Marnie's eyes lit up. She grabbed Adam's hand and pulled him toward the gym.

Inside, the gym was decorated with all kinds of fall décor. Pumpkins and leaves and turkeys, witches, ghosts, and pilgrims all hung from the walls. Dozens of jack-o-lanterns lined the stage, some goofy, some scary. Some of them were even decorated like baseball players dressed in red.

"I made that one," Marnie said, pointing to the largest of the baseball pumpkins.

Adam had arrived too late for the costume contest, but the fifth graders were all dressed up. The whole gym was ablaze with color and costume. It looked—just like a masquerade ball. Adam smiled, remembering Cassandra's fortune. None of the three challenges had been that bad, after all.

Marnie took Adam's hand and led him into the middle of the dance. As the entire fifth-grade class turned to watch Adam Hollinger and Marnie Ellison walk into the dance together, Adam's ears turned so red that they just about matched his baseball uniform.

~ * ~

When Mrs. Hollinger came to pick up Adam from the dance, the car smelled like pizza.

"I ordered a few pies for dinner," Mrs. Hollinger said. "I know it's late, but we wanted to wait for our star pitcher."

Adam smiled.

"Did you have fun at the dance?" Mrs. Hollinger asked as she drove home.

"Yes. Hey, Mom," he said, trying to sound as casual as possible. "Do you think maybe sometime I could invite Marnie over to play?"

Mrs. Hollinger's eyes bulged in the rear-view mirror. "Marnie *Ellison*?" she asked in disbelief. "You sure you're feeling okay?"

"Yes," Adam said.

"Sure," Mrs. Hollinger said. "I think that would be nice."

~ * ~

At home, Zeph howled wildly to greet Adam, which set Sapphie to barking. Before long, they were both making laps around the kitchen. When they finally calmed down, Adam joined the rest of the family in the dining room.

Belle was there with Cassandra, and Courtney, and Mr. and Mrs. Hollinger. The two pizza boxes were stacked on the side of the table. In the middle was a huge cake decorated with a baseball and red lettering that said, *Congratulations Adam, Star Pitcher for the Reds!*

Adam's ears turned red as his whole family gave him another round of applause.

"Good job at the game," Belle said.

"And I'll bet you'll have some great stories to tell the kids at school about how you got that black eye," Cassandra added.

Mr. Hollinger laughed. "I bet it'll impress the girls," he said.

"Or at least, Marnie," Courtney whispered. She gave Adam a sly smile, knowing that he couldn't retaliate with so many people around.

Pizza never tasted so good. Adam had three huge slices before he was full. He ate quietly while everyone else talked.

"Adam," Belle said. "I wanted to thank you for letting me observe you. I'm coming a long way on my thesis. Watching you and Zeph really helped me in my research."

"What are you using it for?" Courtney asked. "Your research, I mean."

"Eventually, I'd like to look into more uses for therapy dogs. Not just for physical therapy, but for emotional therapy as well. For example, dogs can be used as therapy for soldiers, to combat PTSD, and to help wounded warriors."

"That's a good cause," Adam agreed. "I guess I'm glad I was able to help your research."

"Well, then you might want to study me," Courtney told Belle. "You've probably heard about the punishment I have for those shenanigans we pulled during trick-or-treat."

Belle averted her eyes. "Yes," she said. "I've heard that you need to do some volunteer hours."

Courtney nodded. "Mom and Dad want me to volunteer at the nursing home, and they want me to bring Sapphie to help cheer up the old folks who live there. They're even making me take Sapphie to obedience classes before I start volunteering."

"That sounds like it would go good with my research," Belle said.

"Go *well*," Mrs. Hollinger muttered in correction.

"Do you think that I could go along with Courtney on the days she volunteers there? I could even drive her there if you like," Belle asked Mr. and Mrs. Hollinger.

Mr. Hollinger smiled. "That would be great," he said. "It's great for Courtney to have some positive role models."

Belle nodded.

"We're also encouraging her to join some extracurricular activities at school," Mrs. Hollinger said.

"Oh?" asked Cassandra. "And what have you decided to join?"

Courtney smiled. "I'm joining the theater club at school. It's a group that puts on plays. The next play they're working on is a holiday play. It's supposed to be really creative and fun. I'm auditioning for a role next week."

"That sounds great," Cassandra said. "I think you could say I have a little experience with theatre myself. In fact I've been meaning to ask you. My college is putting on a play this winter, and we're looking to fill a role with someone about your age. It's a small part, but it might be good experience for you. What do you think?"

"Mom?" Courtney asked.

"I don't know," Mrs. Hollinger said. "We'll see how things go."

"We'll all get to see Cassandra next weekend at the dress rehearsal for *Macbeth*," Belle said.

Cassandra laughed. "I even stopped wearing my cape around. Did you notice?" She looked at Adam. "I thought you'd be proud of me for dressing normally for once."

Mr. Hollinger looked at Adam, who was finishing a huge piece of cake. "You've been awfully quiet," he said. "Didn't you have a fun time at the dance?"

Courtney smirked, then broke into restrained laughter.

"What's funny?" Mr. Hollinger asked. "Was it something I said?"

"No," Courtney explained. "It's just that Adam isn't saying anything because he doesn't want you to know he went to the dance with Marnie Ellison."

Mr. Hollinger's grinned from ear to ear. Mrs. Hollinger averted her eyes, though she too was smiling. In the kitchen, even Zeph came to the gate and gave Adam a little howl, as if he could understand what was being said.

"All right, all right," Adam said, wondering how red his ears were this time. "I've had a long day. May I be excused?"

"Yes," Mrs. Hollinger said, hiding her smile.

Adam went to the kitchen, lifted Zeph over the safety gate, and went up to his room. He let Zeph curl up on his bed while he showered. Then he changed into his most comfortable pajamas, curled up under his down comforter, and opened his favorite Logan Zephyr comic book while Zeph curled up at his feet. Before he even got to the third page, both Adam and Zeph were sound asleep.

There would be time for more baseball games, and time for Courtney and for Marnie. There would be time for raking leaves, for watching plays, and for schoolwork. But for now, there was just the soft rustle of the leaves outside blowing in the wind, the soft whisper of Zeph's breathing next to Adam, and the most peaceful sleep Adam had had in a long, long time.

~ END ~

About The Author

Val Muller has wanted to be an author since she wrote "The Mystery of Who Killed John Polly" in first grade. A few years ago, her two corgis, Leia and Yoda, talked her into getting serious about her work. They make sure that when she isn't teaching high-school English, she's playing with them, walking them, petting them, feeding them treats, or writing.

Val has published a variety of short stories, plays, and novels for both children and adults. She is an editor at Freedom Forge Press and blogs in her spare time. You can find out more about her at www.ValMuller.com, or follow the Corgi Capers series at www.CorgiCapers.com, and at www.dwbchildrensline.com.

CPSIA information can be obtained
at www.ICGtesting.com
Printed in the USA
FSOW04n2356221216
28772FS

9 780615 707792